A
Harlequin
Romance

OTHER
Harlequin Romances
by MARY WIBBERLEY

COUNTRY
OF THE VINE

by

MARY WIBBERLEY

HARLEQUIN BOOKS   TORONTO
WINNIPEG

Harlequin edition published August 1975

SBN 373-01903-3

Original hard cover edition published in 1975
by Mills & Boon Limited.

Printed in Canada

CHAPTER ONE

THE advertisement wasn't exactly encouraging. It didn't give the impression – or even try to – that this would be the job of anyone's dreams. It was, if anything, couched in discouraging terms. Charlotte Lawson looked at her aunt. 'Oh dear,' she said. 'You thought *this* would be interesting?'

Aunt Emily smiled. 'Well, it is different.'

'It's that all right,' Charlotte agreed.

They were sitting in the comfortable living-room at Emily Lawson's house on the outskirts of Pickerton. Charlotte held the newspaper on her lap, folded to show the advertisement which her aunt had carefully marked, and she looked again at it as she spoke, then read it slowly aloud.

'Responsible young woman to take care of French girl for period of several months. Able to travel. Only those with impeccable references and good knowledge of French need apply. Hand-written letters only to Box No. A177.' She shook her head. 'Impeccable references. Aunt Emily, how would I even get one reference? I've never had a job—'

'My dear, you've lived on a farm all your life, and you worked jolly hard for your parents, God rest their souls – and you're a lot brighter than most of these flighty secretaries—'

'I don't think these people—' Charlotte touched the newsprint lightly, 'would give a jot about the fact that I can milk cows and round up sheep and fill in forms, somehow.'

Her aunt laughed, her blue eyes shrewd in her lined

pleasant face. 'You can but try, can't you? The vicar, and the doctor, and your old headmaster would be only too delighted to give you these impeccable references – come to that, I could give you one! A magistrate is supposed to be a worthy citizen—'

'Oh, Aunt Emily! You are sweet. But that would be cheating! And anyway, what makes you think I'd be interested in the job?'

'My dear,' her aunt said slowly, 'we never know what's round the corner for us. Now I may be an old fogey, but I do occasionally get flashes of something – call it insight if you like or even woman's intuition, but when I read that advert, I knew.'

'Knew what?' Despite everything, Charlotte was intrigued.

'Knew it was for you.'

Charlotte gave her aunt a disbelieving smile, which slowly faded as she saw the seriousness of the other's face. On impulse she went over to hug the older woman. 'Oh, Aunt,' she said. 'You've been so wonderful these past few months since—' she faltered, 'since the accident. I'll write to the box number. Then we'll see.'

'All right,' her aunt agreed. 'And don't think I want to get rid of you. Nothing could be further from the truth. But you're twenty-one now, and it's time you struck out for yourself. It'll do you good. Why, the last time you went anywhere was that holiday with me to Paris—' she stopped abruptly, aware of the expression of pain that crossed her niece's features, then went on hurriedly, too hurriedly: 'I'm sorry, love! What a fool I am—'

'No.' Charlotte shook her head, and now she smiled. 'It's nothing. Really. I'll go and make us a cup of tea before I write that letter. We need one.' She went swiftly

6

out to the kitchen. She wasn't aware of the way Aunt Emily looked at her as she went out, of the deep concern on the older woman's face.

Charlotte filled the kettle. Her hands were very steady. Everything was under control. Two years ago, that holiday in Paris, and there was still the power to hurt her in sudden memories. But not during the day. Only at night, when darkness came, and with it, remembrance. Remembrance of a man she had met for such a brief time. Met and fallen in love with, and in doing so changed from a girl to a woman.

Life was lonely on the farm, and there had been ample time to think about the handsome drifter who had captured her heart in the brief space of a few utterly wonderful days. Three months previously her mother and father had been killed when their car had been struck on a level crossing as they drove to York from their farm on the Yorkshire moors. And since that dreadful day Charlotte had lived with Aunt Emily, only sister of her father, and there had been so many other things to think about that Jared and thoughts of him had been pushed to the back of her mind. Now, a casual remark had brought him startlingly back, and she was frightened. Was he to haunt her again as he had done for so long?

She didn't know. She made the tea and took it in, and she was already mentally composing a letter in answer to that so cool advertisement.

She dreamed of Jared again that night. The bedside clock showed three-thirty when Charlotte woke, her heart beating fast, and sat up to switch on the light. The clock ticked away quietly, and she looked round the quiet room, reassuring herself that she was really here and not – she took a deep breath. Useless to fight it any

7

longer. The image of him was as strong as if he were actually there in the room with her. Yet she was alone. The window was wide open, an owl hooted distantly, and a faint breeze stirred the leaves on the old beech outside the house. From somewhere deep in the house came the sonorous ticks of the grandfather clock, but apart from that everything slept. And Jared was nowhere near. He could be thousands of miles away, certainly not thinking of a shy English girl who had made a fool of herself . . .

Charlotte lay back. Let the thoughts come; they could hurt, and they did, but there was a certain pleasure to them too, seeing again his face, hearing his voice . . .

It had begun at dinner one evening in the small quiet hotel. Aunt Emily and Charlotte shared a table with a young American couple, brother and sister, Jack and Cathie. Towards the end of the meal, Cathie looked across at Charlotte. 'Hey, Charlotte, we're going to a party tonight – why don't we take you?' Charlotte had been about to refuse, but Aunt Emily had replied:

'Why not, child? Don't think you have to stay here with me all the time. I could do with a quiet evening after all that walking today.'

Charlotte, inwardly panicking, had looked desperately at her aunt, and been met with a bland smile. How could you say 'I've never been to parties – I don't know what you do?'

'There y'are,' Jack said, amused. A lanky twenty-five-year-old, he looked as if nothing would ever bother *him*. Both he and his sister were pleasant and easygoing, clearly suitable companions in Aunt Emily's eyes.

'I've nothing to wear,' she said, which was true. Nothing for evening anyway. Cathie laughed.

8

'No problem, honey. It's very casual. Go as you are. That dress is cute.'

An hour later, Charlotte found herself in a taxi with the young Americans, speeding through the Bois de Boulogne at a ridiculous speed. Paris at night was a glittering city. She was nineteen, and she should have been looking forward to going out, but she wasn't. She was scared.

The crumbling mansion was ablaze with light and they were swept into a warm welcoming crowd of people instantly. It was like nothing that had ever happened before, the noise, the colour, the sheer variety of what seemed like hundreds of men and women of all types. Young and old, and some dressed like hippies, others in evening dress, yet more dressed casually. One woman, easily in her forties, was dressed in blue jeans and dark sweater. And round her neck was a diamond collar that if it was real was worth thousands. And it *looked* real . . . They looked after Charlotte at first, but soon, inevitably, were drawn into a circle of young Americans, and somehow she got left out. She stood in a quiet corner watching, deafened by the music from a gigantic stereo, clutching a glass of wine as if her life depended on it, praying for the hours to pass swiftly. She didn't even know *where* she was . . .

'You're too beautiful to be alone. Where's your escort? Is he bigger than me?' The voice was deep, and held laughter. And Charlotte looked up, and in that moment of time her life changed.

The man stood in front of her, and he was big, and deeply tanned, and smiling. She smiled back, because she couldn't help herself. She shook her head gently. She had seen films occasionally, and she knew that everyone talked in witty fashion at parties, and that she should reply with something clever – but she couldn't have done that, not for anything.

'I'm alone,' she said. 'I came with an American couple, but they seem to have vanished.' He overwhelmed her. Why should anyone like *him* stop to talk to her? She had never seen such an attractive man in her life. Over six feet tall, broad-shouldered, his face dark and hawklike with fascinating tawny eyes under thick level brows, a nose that might have been broken at some time, a wide well-shaped mouth, good teeth – because he was laughing, and his teeth were white and strong, and he said:

'Then it's my lucky day, isn't it? Come on, let's grab a drink and talk, *then* we'll dance.' He was taking charge in a quite unsubtle way, and Charlotte, to her surprise, found that it was a delightful sensation.

Within minutes they were sitting on the uncarpeted stairs, each holding full glasses, and with a loaded plate of ham and olives and onions in front of them. The noise was no less intense, but somehow they were apart from it now, and the man, so close beside Charlotte that she felt his hard muscular body against hers, said: 'I'm Jared. Who are you?'

'Charlotte. How – how did you know I was English?' she asked shyly.

He laughed. 'How did I know? I just *did*.'

'Oh.'

'Come on, eat up. This ham is delicious. Then tell me all about yourself.' He must be teasing. She looked down at her lap. If only she could indulge in small talk, the light badinage she had heard from the noise swirling round her in the room before. That was what this man wanted – not to hear her life story. In a minute he would go away, and she probably wouldn't see him again. So there was no point in keeping him here against his will.

She turned slightly sideways to look at him, and was aware of the faint but disturbing tang of some spicy after-shave lotion. He wore a deep blue shirt, unbuttoned nearly to his waist. It was a hot night.

'Look,' she said. 'It's very kind of you to rescue me from the corner, but I'm sure you've got friends here—'

'Trying to get rid of me? Hmm, I see.' He gave her a mock serious glance from those startlingly golden sherry eyes. 'That's *nice*. I haven't even made a pass at you yet.'

She had to smile. There was something irresistible about his expression. 'That's better,' he said. 'Do you know how beautiful you are when you smile?' She knew she was going pink. She could do nothing about it. No man had ever spoken to her like he did before. It was exciting in a way. She felt breathless.

He stood up and held out his hand. 'Come on,' he said. 'Let's go for a walk in the gardens. We can't talk here.'

'The ham—' she began, protesting faintly, but already his hand was over hers and he was pulling her along, gently down the stairs, stepping over the plate carefully, leaving their empty glasses beside it.

'Damn the ham,' he answered. 'Let's talk. We can get some more when we come back if that's gone.'

Charlotte turned restlessly in bed. She could remember quite clearly, even now, after the space of two years, her feelings at the time as Jared had led her out of a doorway and into the dark garden. She should have been nervous – he was a complete stranger– but she hadn't been. Instinct had told her to trust him. Instinct had been right. The memories flooded back, and she couldn't have stopped them if she had wanted.

'Mind the path, there are stones. You don't want to

trip,' and as he said it, he put his arm round her. The house was left behind them, the lights flooded out, but didn't reach their part of the path, and the racket of the over-loud music was muted by the distance, so that it became almost pleasant.

'Where are we going?' she asked.

'To look at the ducks, of course,' he seemed faintly surprised. 'Why else would I bring you out?'

And suddenly, quite suddenly, Charlotte realized that she was enjoying herself. One evening of her holiday, an unwilling partygoer, and she would never see him again after tonight, but it didn't matter, because he was a most fascinating man, and she was in a darkened garden with him, and she trusted him completely.

She laughed. 'Of *course*,' she said. 'The ducks! *That's* why I came to this party – just to see them.'

'We should have brought the food out. They'd enjoy the ham, though I'm not so sure about the onions. Do ducks like onions?' he spoke as if deeply interested.

'I don't know. I must try ours with a few when I get back home. Perhaps fried ones, you never know.'

'You have ducks?' he seemed impressed, and somehow, the next minute, Charlotte was telling him about the farm, and now there was no constraint, no forcing it, he was genuinely interested, she could tell.

They stood by the dark expanse of lake, still and cool, with weeping willows trailing their leaves in the water, and only the occasional rustling of feathers to betray the sleeping birds. She shivered because it was colder there by the edge, and Jared said: 'Do you want to go back?'

'No, not yet.' She looked up at him. His face was shadowy, a grey blur, and he was much taller than her, and from nearby came the sound of whispered voices, and muffled laughter. They were not alone, it seemed.

'Good. I like it here. It's peaceful. Very peaceful. And we won't be disturbed if I—' he didn't finish the sentence. He bent his head and kissed her.

Charlotte had never been kissed before. She had imagined it happening, of course, had wondered what it must be like to have a man kiss you. But she hadn't known the reality. It was simply beautiful. There were no other words to describe the experience. Strong and tender, his arms were round her as if they would never let her go, and she responded instinctively to his mouth.

And even when the kiss was over, the magic continued. It continued for three days, during which time Charlotte knew that she had fallen deeply in love with the dark mystery man who had come into her life so unexpectedly.

She put her hand to her mouth. It had all ended so suddenly. Ended with ten red roses and a brief note delivered to her hotel when she had been waiting for him to phone on the last day of her holiday. But she had sworn never to think of that any more. She had decided to put it all out of her mind and remember only the happiness. Easier said than done. Aunt Emily had been a brick. Charlotte had looked back at the airport as their plane left Paris. Her eyes ached with unshed tears, her throat was dry. It was all over. She didn't even know his surname, or where he came from, or how old he was. She knew only his name: Jared. And knew only the bittersweet memories of kisses freely given.

She slept little during the rest of the night, and when morning came, she posted a letter to the box number in the newspaper.

The envelope was heavy, the paper more like parchment than notepaper. Charlotte looked at the spidery writing

13

with its Gallic flavour. The writer had scorned to use her stamped addressed envelope apparently.

'Well, go on, open it,' her aunt said impatiently. 'Let's see what they say.'

Charlotte smiled. 'I haven't drunk my tea yet.' Then, seeing her aunt's expression, 'Oh, all right.

'Dear Miss Lawson,' she read aloud. 'Will you please arrange to attend an interview at the Royal Station Hotel in York on Tuesday next, at two p.m. Ask for Madame Grenier.' It was signed: 'Heloise Grenier.' There was no address at the top of the page, merely the date. Charlotte passed the letter over to Aunt Emily, who read it slowly again, as if to find subtler shades of meaning that her niece might have missed.

'Hmm,' she commented. 'Like the advert, brief and to the point. Tuesday – that's tomorrow. Now, what will you wear?'

Despite herself, Charlotte experienced a prickle of excitement. 'I'm frightened,' she admitted. 'Isn't that strange?'

'Hardly,' her aunt said, 'seeing that you've never been interviewed before. But I shouldn't worry. I told you – I've got a *feeling* about this. Now, let's see, we'll go to York in the morning and have lunch, then you go off to your interview and I'll meet you in the hotel lounge afterwards. We don't know how long it'll take, so I'll order myself coffee and read a book—'

'About five minutes, I should imagine,' Charlotte answered. 'I'll bet she's a real dragon.'

'Rubbish!' Her aunt looked severely at her. 'She'll probably be quite charming. I wonder how many others are being interviewed?' she added thoughtfully. Her eyes went up and down Charlotte's slender figure, ~~pped~~ at her niece's face, and then she nodded. ~~yes.'~~

'Hmm, yes, what?' Charlotte was intrigued.

'I think a touch of make-up wouldn't come amiss—' then as Charlotte was about to protest, she added quickly: 'Just a *touch*, love, I know you don't like the stuff, but I've always fancied myself as a make-up artist, and you look so young—'

'I am young!' Charlotte laughingly replied. 'You'll be telling me next you want to do something with my hair.'

'Yes, well, I was about to come to that too. Now it's lovely as it is, all short and blonde and wavy, but if we could just put in a couple of curlers—'

'No,' Charlotte said, but faintly, for there was that look on Aunt Emily's face, and it was the kind of look she wore when she was about to get her own way. She sighed. What did it matter? Aunt Emily was so good, it would do no harm to indulge her little whims for once. 'All right, you win,' she said, 'I give in.'

Her aunt smiled. 'Good,' she said. 'Now I'll just pop out to the chemist in the village. I won't be long . . .'

Charlotte sat patiently at her dressing table. Tuesday morning, ten a.m., an hour's drive to York ahead of them, and it was all planned. Her aunt had taken over with great efficiency, and Charlotte looked in the mirror, and then closed her eyes obediently at Emily's command. She hid a smile. The older woman was really enjoying herself. It was almost worth it.

'There, that's it. Just a touch of blue eye-shadow. Too much is vulgar during the day, but you have such lovely deep-set eyes, it's a shame not to enhance them a little.'

Charlotte kept her eyes closed. It might be interesting to see what transformation, if any, had been wrought, when her aunt had finished. She had come back the previous day loaded up with bottles and jars from the local chemists. There was even a bottle of perfume in the collection. Charlotte hadn't even looked at it yet. She had never used perfume in her life.

'There, you can look now. How's that?' Her aunt stepped back to admire her handiwork, and Charlotte opened her eyes. For just a split second she didn't recognize herself. Then she laughed.

'Is that *me*? What *have* you done?'

'Something you should have learnt long ago. Given nature a little helping hand.' Charlotte had good bones, high cheekbones, oval face, gently rounded chin, and her golden hair, newly washed and curled, softly framed her face. A touch of pencil to skilfully darken her well arched eyebrows, pink lipstick on her full mouth, eyes glowing darkly blue. She didn't realize that she was beautiful, she only knew that she felt good, and turned round to thank her aunt and tell her so.

Aunt Emily saw the beauty there, the soft gentle radiance that could so easily remain hidden, and she was well satisfied with her work.

'Right,' she said briskly, 'let's get ready. Mind how you put that dress on, don't disturb your hair or make-up. Want any help?'

'No, thanks, I'll manage,' Charlotte assured her. 'I'll not take a minute.'

And then, within half an hour, they were on their way to York. It was a gloriously sunny day and Aunt Emily sang as she drove along, which was always a good sign, for she tended to get slightly impatient with other road users usually.

Charlotte smiled at her. 'You're very good to bring me,' she said. 'I could have got the bus, I know Tuesday's a busy day for you.'

'Huh, it's only the Guild this afternoon. They can

manage without me for one week. Can't have you arriving all dusty from that bus. No, I'm enjoying myself, dear, don't you worry.'

They ate lunch at a restaurant near the hotel, and lingered over coffee so that at a quarter to two, Emily said: 'We'll go now, and I'll get settled in the lounge, and you can make a good impression by being precisely one minute early.'

'Yes, Aunt,' said Charlotte obediently, but with a trace of impish humour in her voice. 'I don't know about being a make-up artist, you should have been a stage manager, you seem to be managing my interview very well up to now.'

'I'm glad you think so,' her aunt agreed graciously. 'I do my best.'

She had a moment of panic as she approached the receptionist. What if they should look at her blankly and say they had never heard of Madame Grenier?

She ran her tongue over dry lips and asked the fateful question. And the next minute she was being whisked up in a lift, accompanied by an affable man who guided her to a door, knocked, waited a moment, listening, then said: 'You can go in, miss.'

A woman sat facing the door. She was elderly, but it was difficult to see her face, for the window was behind her, leaving her in shadow. Her voice was cool.

'Miss Lawson? Good afternoon. Please sit down.'

'Good afternoon.' As Charlotte sat down in an easy chair, her nervousness dropped from her like a cloak. It was strange to feel like that. Perhaps something in the woman's autocratic manner did it – the way she sat, straight-backed and intimidating in the chair. She intended putting Charlotte at a disadvantage. She could not know that Charlotte had only come to please her aunt, not because she was desperate to get the job. It made a subtle difference, and suddenly Charlotte was no longer afraid. She tilted her chin and met the other's glance with her own direct gaze. And waited for her to speak.

The older woman gave a slight nod, a mere inclination of the head. It was almost as if she acknowledged Charlotte's thoughts. 'Now, miss,' she began. 'Tell me about yourself.'

There was so little to tell, and no use at all in pretending anything. Charlotte didn't want to try. She told the older woman of her life on the farm, of her parents' accident, and that she was now living with her aunt in a village on the Yorkshire moors. The woman listened in silence. Charlotte finished: 'I have never been employed by anyone, as I always worked on the farm, so I have no job qualifications at all. I can only offer you references from my doctor, vicar, and old headmaster.'

'And why did you apply for this post?' The voice was cool, giving nothing away. Was this a typical interview? Charlotte wondered. Was this how prospective employers behaved? Something told her that this woman was a law unto herself. No use telling half truths, pretending it was something she really wanted.

'My aunt read your advertisement. It was she who told me to write to you. She thought it would be a good post.' She had probably finished her chance now. For some reason she didn't care. And it was therefore almost a shock when the old lady smiled.

'I like your honesty,' she answered. 'Yes, I like that. One other young lady that I interviewed this morning told me that she had always wanted to care for a child – what a stupid response! It didn't fool me.' And then, almost in the same breath, she added: '*Vous semblez très jeune, mademoiselle. Quelle âge avez-vous?*'

It was calculated to confuse. Charlotte had a good knowledge of French and had been waiting subconsciously for something of the kind. Without hesitation she answered: '*J'ai vingt-et-un ans, madame.*' And she smiled.

'*Bien!*' She switched again to English. 'Your accent is well enough. Tell me, Miss Lawson, when would you be able to begin your duties?'

For a moment Charlotte looked blankly at the older woman. Then she found her voice. 'But you have others to interview?' It was all too sudden.

'No. I have seen three young women today. I made yours the last appointment because I liked your handwriting — I find that a very interesting guide to character — I have told the others that I will let them know. I do not need to tell you, for I have decided. How soon can you begin?'

Charlotte swallowed. 'As soon as you like.'

'I wish you to meet my granddaughter as soon as possible. Say tomorrow? I will send a car to your house for you at ten in the morning. And if everything is satisfactory, I would like you to begin next Sunday.' She sensed that the interview was over. Just like that. It was as if the woman had lost interest in her. Charlotte stood up. 'Thank you, Madame Grenier,' she said. 'I'll be ready at ten in the morning. *Au revoir.*'

'*Au revoir,* Miss Lawson.'

She went out in a daze. Aunt Emily would never believe it — or would she? Charlotte went down to tell her.

CHAPTER TWO

THE car, a sleek black Daimler, arrived at five to ten the following morning. Aunt Emily was looking out of the living-room window, and called Charlotte to her. 'It's got a chauffeur,' she hissed, as if the man might hear her – 'and I'll swear there's someone in the back!'

Charlotte dared a quick peep. 'Oh! It looks like Madame Grenier,' she said. 'What shall we do?'

'Ask her in for a coffee, of course,' retorted Aunt Emily. 'What else?' and went to the door. Charlotte waited. She was making a big mistake, she knew that now. She should never have listened to her aunt in the first place . . .

'It won't take a moment, *madame*,' Aunt Emily was coming in, ushering the old woman in front of her, and now, for the first time, Charlotte was able to see her new – her *first* – employer. She was probably seventy, hawk-nosed, her white hair swept severely back from her face into a bun at her neck. She wore a fur coat, although the day was warm, and a long black skirt. Eccentric but extremely dignified, she swept in, her eyes missing nothing, Charlotte would have sworn, noting every item of the too old furniture her aunt so loved.

'It is extremely kind of you, Miss Lawson,' said Madame Grenier. 'Good morning,' this to Charlotte, who only resisted curtseying by sheer will power. She had that effect on you.

'Good morning, *madame*. I'll make the coffee, Aunt Emily.' And Charlotte escaped to the kitchen before her aunt could reply. Not that she seemed inclined to, she was sitting down, asking the older woman to do the same, already talking. She could hear the voices faintly as she prepared coffee in the percolator, and bit her lip. Knowing her aunt as she did, she could imagine that the Frenchwoman would be getting a subtle grilling. Emily Lawson hadn't been a magistrate nearly thirty years for nothing. The gentle exterior hid a formidable personality. She would undoubtedly be assuring herself of the suitability of the post for her niece. Charlotte put her hand to her mouth to stifle sudden laughter. What would Madame Grenier make of *that*? She was soon to find out.

As they drove along the country lanes a half hour or so later, the Frenchwoman said to Charlotte: 'Your aunt is very concerned for your welfare, is she not?'

'Yes.' She wondered what was coming next.

'That is good. I like that. So many people nowadays do not care.' She took a sharp sideways glance at Charlotte sitting beside her in the back of the roomy vehicle. 'That is partly why I came with Yves this morning. Your references to your aunt yesterday intrigued me. I have assured her of your welfare, and I am sure she is satisfied.'

'Yes, I'm sure she is,' Charlotte murmured, and managed a smile. So everything had gone off all right. They were travelling swiftly, but the driver seemed to know the road well, and Charlotte, who had never been in such a luxurious car, began to relax. She wondered what the child would be like. She didn't know her age or her name, and she was certain that this meeting would be to see if they both got on together.

'Do you know where we are going?' asked Madame Grenier.

'No. To the hotel in York?'

'No. I merely took a room yesterday for the interviews. We are staying at a house a few miles outside

21

York, Redvale Manor.'

Charlotte couldn't hide her surprise. One of York-shire's statelier mansions, Redvale Manor was a house of great beauty and charm. She had seen photographs of it, but never the actual place. And now she was going there for a day, or at least for a few hours. It began to seem as if Aunt Emily's intuition had been right on target.

They swept up a wide tree-lined drive that curved gradually round, hiding the house effectively from the road, and the gaze of passing cars. It was even more beautiful in reality than on photograph. Charlotte took a deep breath. This was more than she had bargained for. Madame Grenier had made a bad mistake choosing her for this post. She looked down at the plain blue dress, the same that she had worn for her interview on the previous day. It was her best one – her only one, come to that. Living on a farm which had been remote enough to discourage casual visitors, Charlotte had always dressed in trousers and sweaters, and never been interested in clothes. But she might have to buy some, she realized that now. She sighed inwardly. Money wasn't the prob-lem. It was a question of choice. She had no idea of fashion at all. Yet this formidable Frenchwoman would hardly be expected to understand that.

And then they were stopping in front of the gracious red brick house, lit by the sun, so that it glowed, and the windows sparkled, and in an upstairs room, a curtain moved slightly, then was still. Someone was watching them get out of the car. Charlotte wondered if it was the girl.

The driver held the door, and she looked at him. She had expected a middle-aged man, but he was young, probably in his late twenties, and good-looking in a dark gipsyish fashion, and he looked at Charlotte in a way

22

that made her go warm. Madame Grenier swept up the steps, and called in French 'Leave the car there, Yves.'

'*Oui, madame,*' he answered. But his eyes were still on Charlotte, and suddenly he smiled. She smiled back, and then turned away, and followed the old woman up to the house. So that was Yves, the chauffeur, and Charlotte didn't know what to make of him at all. He was quite unlike Jared. With that thought came a pang, a slight ache of the heart, and she took a deep breath and tried to dismiss it. She must try to forget Jared now. Only that was going to be difficult, as she found out a short while later when she sat in a beautiful drawing-room drinking coffee with Madame Grenier.

A maid had brought in a trolley and been told to leave it, as they would look after themselves. They were alone, and Charlotte sensed that she was in a way on trial. There had been no mention of the girl she was to look after. The conversation was general, the older woman telling Charlotte that she had been staying at Redvale Manor for two months, and was soon to return to France. Charlotte had poured out their coffee at her new employer's request, and then Madame Grenier said: 'You have a passport, Miss Lawson?'

'Yes. I had a holiday in Fance with my aunt two years ago.'

'Ah! Good. Then you will be prepared to return there with my granddaughter?'

She should have known. Perhaps, subconsciously, she had already done so when she had read the words 'able to travel' in the advertisement. Even so, the words sent a slight shock through her. She managed to hide it.

'To France? Of – course.' Only the merest thread of hesitation as she replied. Not to Paris, please not to Paris, she prayed inwardly.

The old woman smiled. 'You are perhaps curious to know whereabouts in France you will be going?'

'Why, yes, of course.' And Charlotte smiled. Autocratic and regal her employer might be, yet there was something about her that told Charlotte that she could be warm-hearted and kind.

'We have a vineyard in central France. My grandchild, Marie, is heiress to half of it when she is of age, and it is a beautiful place. We will be leaving in two weeks. You and Marie will travel by car and boat. I will fly as I am a poor traveller – the quicker the better for me.' The dignified face relaxed slightly at Charlotte's expression. 'Ah yes, you are wondering something?'

Charlotte shook her head. There were several questions that presented themselves, but it certainly wasn't her place to ask. The main one: Why didn't they all fly? The second: Would Yves be driving them?

They were answered almost immediately. 'No, *mademoiselle*, you are merely being polite. But you must ask yourself why do we not travel together? *Eh bien*, it is simple. Marie's parents – my son and his wife – were killed in a plane crash one year ago. She is not permitted to fly anywhere *at all*, whereas I am old and can please myself. Yves is very reliable. I trust him implicitly. He will look after you both well. His knowledge of English is limited, but he and Marie get on well, and I am sure you will find that you do too. The present owner of the vineyard is my nephew, Monsieur de Marais. When Marie is grown up, he and she will share it.'

Charlotte nodded. 'I see, *madame*.'

'Your duties, after we are there, will be to be companion to Marie – and of course to help her with her English. She is a clever child, but rather delicate, as you will see.'

'Will I meet her today, *madame*?'

'Of course. Soon I will send for her. But first I wished us to have our little talk. We will have lunch later, and then perhaps a walk round the gardens. And then Yves will take you home to your aunt.'

She leaned back in her chair and closed her eyes, as if tired. Charlotte waited silently. Her mind was a turmoil of mixed emotions. Companion to an heiress! She imagined Aunt Emily's face at that little bit of information, and smiled slightly to herself. Her aunt would probably nod and say something like: 'I'm not a bit surprised!'

'Good!' The old woman's voice startled Charlotte out of her daydream.

'I'm sorry?' She was puzzled.

'You have that quality of silence that I admire – by that I mean that you do not feel it necessary to talk all the time. I feel we may get on well with each other, *mademoiselle*.'

Charlotte smiled gently. 'I have been used to being alone most of my life, *madame*. I am not used to doing a lot of talking.'

'Marie is a lonely child, Miss Lawson. Perhaps you will understand her. She can be moody. Maybe, if she had a brother or sister,' there came an eloquent shrug. '*Hélas*, that is not possible now. But you will be good for her, I am sure.' She pointed to the fireplace. 'Be so good as to press that bell, *mademoiselle*.'

Charlotte obeyed, and a minute later the maid came in.

'Brown, please bring Marie in to us.'

'Yes, ma'am,' the maid gave Charlotte a long look and went out.

There was a waiting silence for a few moments, then the door opened again, and a child walked in. Her eyes met Charlotte's, and she was startled to see in them a certain lost look. The girl was nine or ten, tall and thin with long dark hair down her back. The eyes that met Charlotte's were a clear light blue. She was dressed in a short summer dress of white, with a grass smear on the lap, and on her feet were white sandals.

'*Tiens*, Marie, could you not have changed your dress?'

'*Mais, Grand'mère, j'étais—*'

'English, Marie. Please speak English in front of Miss Lawson.'

'I was playing, Grandmother.' She said it slowly as if the language were very strange to her, and the old woman looked at Charlotte, and clicked her tongue.

'Never mind, child. Come here and be introduced.'

The handshake was formal. The girl had good manners. She gave Charlotte a smile, and a sudden warmth lit her rather plain features. 'I am pleased to meet you, Miss Lawson,' she said haltingly.

'And I am pleased to meet you, Marie,' Charlotte answered.

'Good. Now go and change your dress. Then come back for lunch.'

'Yes, Grandmother.' With a last quick look at Charlotte, the girl ran out. Madame Grenier sighed.

'She will need training, that one, before she is a young lady. She prefers animals to humans, I am quite sure. No doubt she has been feeding the rabbits, not playing at all.'

Charlotte laughed, unaware of the older woman's eyes on her. 'Then I'm sure we'll get on well.'

'I hope you do, I really hope you do.' The small sigh that followed the words was a mere whisper, but Charlotte wondered at it.

They ate lunch in a large long dining-room, just the three of them, and it was delicious, from the smoked salmon to the sweet of fresh strawberries and thick cream. Afterwards, Madame Grenier looked at the fob watch she wore on her black dress, and frowned.

'Oh dear, I intended to show you round the gardens now, but I really must make some phone calls. Marie, will you show Miss Lawson around for me?'

'Yes, Grandmother.' The girl looked at Charlotte. 'You wish to go now, miss?'

'If that's all right, I'd like to very much.' She wondered if the old woman really had phone calls to make—or if this was a way to let them get to know one another. It seemed quite possible. And suddenly, she didn't know why, it was important to Charlotte that she and the girl who was to be her charge should get on well. She didn't understand it herself. She just knew that this post was assuming greater importance with every minute that passed.

Perhaps it had been the look in the girl's eyes. A look that Charlotte had understood only too well.

They went out of the front door, down the steps, and Charlotte looked round at her surroundings for a moment in silence. 'Marie,' she said, 'Madame Grenier tells me there are rabbits here. Will you show them to me?'

'You *like* rabbits?' She sounded surprised, making Charlotte laugh.

'I have lived on a farm all my life. I like all animals — but if I have a favourite, I suppose I would have to say dogs.'

'Ah — *les chiens*! *Pardon*, miss! I forget sometimes.'

'That is all right, Marie. You speak English very well.'

The girl pulled a little face. 'Grand'mère insists that I do. I prefer to speak French, of course.'

'Of course. And I would like to practise my French sometimes too.' And Charlotte grinned impishly at her young companion. 'Perhaps, just *occasionally*, we can speak a little French?'

Marie laughed. 'Occasionally, yes. Come, I will show to you the rabbits.'

They were behind the house, in a large wire enclosed run, half a dozen or so, pink eyes watchful as the two girls approached. Then, as if recognizing Marie, two ran forward to the wire netting, and she knelt down and touched their noses, then looked up at Charlotte, her eyes shining.

'They know me, miss.'

'I can see that,' Charlotte agreed smilingly. 'But you won't be able to take them back with you when you return to France.'

'Ah no, but there I have my two dogs waiting for me to return.' The girl stood up. 'And perhaps it is better that the rabbits stay here. My two dogs would eat them.' She looked at the rabbits, then turned away. 'Come, we will walk round now. Then we will return to grandmother and tell her that we get on well enough, for I feel that is why she has sent us off together.'

Charlotte looked at her. There was no doubt about the girl's intelligence. The words were said quite calmly and logically.

'Do you go to school, Marie?' she asked.

The girl shook her head. 'No. I have a tutor.' She pulled her face. 'She is very strict.'

'But it is important that you learn your lessons.'

'Perhaps. But it has been nice here. No—' she hesitated – 'I do not know the English word – *devoir*?'

'Homework?' Charlotte suggested.

'Yes, homework, that is it. I can read my books instead.'

'Ah, you like reading too? So do I. We'll have to compare notes.'

'*Comment*? What does "compare notes" mean, please?'

'Oh, talk about books, I mean – see if we have read the same ones.'

'Yes, I see.' Marie nodded wisely. 'I like the adventure stories – and travel tales – things like that.'

'Hmm,' Charlotte was going over her collection mentally. 'Would you like me to bring a few from home when I come here? It might be fun to try and read in English. And in return, I'll promise to read some of yours in French – that will be like homework for *me*.'

Marie suddenly started to laugh and took hold of Charlotte's hand in an impulsive gesture. 'I think I will like you!' she announced. 'Of course, please let me see some of your books. Oh, what a pity you are not my tutor, instead of Mademoiselle Lucy.'

The gardens were extensive, well tended and beautiful, and nearly an hour had passed when at last they returned to the house to find Madame Grenier waiting for them.

They drank coffee in the drawing-room and talked, and when Marie went out to bring some books to show Charlotte, her grandmother said: 'I am pleased with your visit today, Miss Lawson. My granddaughter's happiness is important to me. And I can see that you have a certain empathy with each other.'

'We've discovered that we have one or two common interests, *madame*.'

'Yes, I am sure. Well, soon it will be time for you to go. And I will send the car for you on Sunday – after lunch – will that be suitable?'

'Yes, of course.'

'Perhaps your aunt would like to come here with you,

and see you settled in.' A faint trace of a smile accompanied the word.

'She would love to, I'm sure, *madame*.'

'Good. That is arranged, then. On Sunday you will commence your duties.'

It was rather a sad moment when the time came for Aunt Emily to leave on Sunday evening. Charlotte went out to the car with her, and they stood talking for a few minutes. Yves was nowhere to be seen, and they were alone. Emily squeezed Charlotte's hand. 'Madame Grenier can be formidable,' she whispered, 'but she's a very charming woman inside.'

'I know,' answered Charlotte. 'You were right about that advert – I think.'

Aunt Emily laughed. 'There you are!' she said. 'Told you so.' She looked around her, to the twilight that was turning everything to silver grey shadow. The bright lights shone out from the house, bathing them in warm gold. 'You'll phone me when you can of course – let me know how everything's going?'

'Of course,' Charlotte hugged her, 'and thank you for everything.' And Yves appeared silently from the back of the house. He was an impressive figure in smart dark uniform, and the light caught his face as he came up and said, in French: 'Is Madame ready to leave?'

'I think so, Yves, thank you.' He no longer made her feel uneasy, as he had done, unaccountably, on that first occasion. He seemed harmless enough, and his manners were good. Charlotte kissed her aunt warmly. 'Bye-bye, love. See you soon.'

She watched them go, the tail lights dwindling down the drive to vanish with a final wink and blink into the darkness of the trees. Then with a little sigh, she went back into the house. This was it, the beginning of a new life. She couldn't help wondering if she was going to be happy.

Yves drove them to York the following week, on Wednesday, and Charlotte helped Marie choose some coats and shoes and dresses to add to her already extensive wardrobe. She was aware that it was a compliment on Madame Grenier's part to trust her with such a task, and she was determined not to let her down. Marie had strong ideas of her own regarding clothes, as Charlotte soon discovered, and her intentions were not quite as easy to keep as she had thought.

'No, Marie, honestly, those shoes don't suit you,' Charlotte assured the girl as she tried on a pair of brightly striped clumsy-looking clogs and looked admiringly at herself in a mirror. Charlotte's heart sank. She could imagine the old woman's expression if they returned with *those*!

A ten-year-old French girl, and already with strong views on fashion! And that thought inspired Charlotte. In her calmest voice – almost casual – she said: 'As a matter of fact, they make your legs look rather plump, whereas these—' and she picked up a pair of smart red ones – 'make you seem like a teenager.'

There was a pause – a doubtful pause – then Marie said: 'Hmm, perhaps I will try those red ones on again, Charlotte. Pass them to me, will you, please.' Nothing showed on Charlotte's face. Inwardly she breathed a sigh of relief. She was learning. It would perhaps take time, but she was beginning to find out the best way to treat this young French girl who had a mind of her own hidden under that gentle exterior.

Yves took them to Scarborough on Saturday. And she and Marie wandered along the front thoroughly enjoying themselves, eating ice creams and marzipan sweets from a shop on the promenade, playing the fruit machines, laughing whether they won or lost. Yves accompanied them, because he said Madame Grenier had told him to. Charlotte wondered whether this was in fact so, and while she and Marie were playing a game of football in one of the amusement arcades, she said: 'Does Yves always come with you when you go out?' He had been with them on Wednesday, but that was understandable as there was a lot of shopping to carry. Marie shrugged.

'Oh yes. Grandmama thinks someone may try to kidnap me or something.' Said in matter-of-fact tones, and for a moment Charlotte thought she was joking – then saw her face, and knew she wasn't. It jolted her. She looked round to where Yves waited, feeding pennies into a one-armed bandit. He might not have been with them at all.

'Oh, Charlotte, your face! I have shocked you, perhaps?'

'No, of course not.' Charlotte smiled warmly at her. She was begining to realize something of the little girl's isolation. Perhaps there was no fun in being an heiress after all. She had a sudden remembrance of something Madame Grenier had told her about the vineyard.

'Is your uncle married?' she asked. He might have young children . . .

'Uncle Zhar? Oh no!' Marie laughed in great amusement. 'He is a spinster.'

Charlotte joined the laughter. 'You mean a bachelor!'

'Yes, a bachelor. Aren't I silly? A spinster is a lady, isn't it?'

'Yes. He lives at the vineyard, does he?'

Marie sighed. 'Yes. Only since – since a year ago.'
Charlotte bit her lip, wishing she had not asked. She had

only done so to change the subject from talk of kidnapping, but she had no wish to distress the girl. She went on hurriedly: 'It will be nice to see him again, I'm sure.'

'Oh yes. We get on well enough, he and I. But—' and here she shrugged, 'he does not really want to run a vineyard. He prefers to travel about. He has many girlfriends,' and she rolled her eyes and grinned mischievously.

'Oh, I see.' Time to change the subject. 'We'd better move on, I think those boys want to use this machine, Marie. Come, let's go along the beach for a while.'

'All right.' Marie was always agreeable. And they went out of the arcade into bright sunshine, and Yves followed them.

'You would like Uncle Zhar, I think,' confided Marie as they walked along the dry golden sand, and Charlotte imagined that he had been forgotten. 'He is very dark and tall and handsome.' And she sighed. 'I am sorry he is my uncle, I would like to marry him when I grow up.'

'Never mind, I'm sure you'll meet someone equally nice,' Charlotte said, straight-faced.

'Perhaps. But he makes me laugh – oh, he is *funny*! You see – he will make you laugh too. And he is strong! He can pick me up and throw me to the ceiling—' Charlotte was only half listening to this eulogy. Understandable for a child with few playmates – if any at all – to idolize a relative. She let the girl ramble on happily as they walked along the beach, Yves casually near, but not too near, so that whatever they said was private. This Uncle Zhar – what a strange name! – sounded more of a playboy than anything else. Marie seemed convinced that Charlotte would like him. She herself was not so sure.

A small incident as they returned to the car served to accentuate the differences in Marie's life from that of a normal child. Two youths were playing with a ball on the beach and one sent it flying towards Charlotte so that she had to duck to avoid it. It landed at her feet and one of the youths – about nineteen – dashed up laughing and called, 'Want a game?'

'No, thanks—' she began, and he grabbed her arm.

'Don't be snooty—' That was all he said, because Yves was there, and knocked his arm away. The youth looked at him sharply, about to say something, then saw Yves's face. His eyes were very cold. The youth pulled a face, muttered: 'Keep your hair on,' grabbed the ball, and swaggered away.

Charlotte felt suddenly angry. She said to Marie: 'Walk on, please, I want to talk to Yves.' Then she turned to him, and said quietly, in French, 'You had no need to do that. I can look after myself. He was only a boy.'

Yves looked at her. No expression showed on his face. 'I have my instructions,' he said calmly.

'Yes, to look after Marie. Not me.'

'You too, *mademoiselle*.' And he smiled slowly. 'You are with her, therefore I look after you as well.'

Marie was standing nearby, watching them. Charlotte decided not to pursue the matter. She didn't want an argument in front of the girl, and it wasn't important anyway. It had been only a slight incident, better forgotten.

She shrugged. 'Very well. But remember, I'm not a child.'

'I am well aware of that, *mademoiselle*.' The look he gave her said more than his words. Charlotte turned away to go to the girl. Outwardly calm, inwardly she was shaking. There was something about Yves that dis-

34

turbed her, but she didn't know what it was.

A week later they left Yorkshire and began the journey that was to take them to France. Charlotte turned round and took a last look at the gracious old house before it was hidden in the trees. Madame Grenier had left earlier that morning, to catch a plane. She would be at the vineyard before them.

Marie sat beside her in the back of the car. Yves drove, and his manner was correct and formal. Since the incident on the beach at Scarborough, Charlotte had seen little of him, and had begun to think that it had all been her imagination. She hoped so.

They were driving to London, stopping overnight there, and going by car ferry the following day. There would be one night in Paris – not in a hotel, but in the family apartment near the Champs-Elysées – and then they would go on to the vineyard the following morning. Charlotte sat back in her comfortable seat.

Everything was arranged, all planned to a nicety, working smoothly. Nothing like this had ever happened before. She had worked hard all her life for very little reward, save the satisfaction of helping her parents. And all that had ended so tragically a short while before. And now there was nothing. Nothing to show for those quiet busy years on a farm, save enough money to last a while. She looked out of the window. It was up to her to make this job a success. It was only temporary, perhaps for a few months, maybe a year, and when it was over she would return to England. But for that time she would have the opportunity to live a life with very wealthy people, to taste something completely different from anything she had ever known. It would all be experience. She looked at Marie, who sat quietly beside her. She would do her best for the girl, she knew that.

At first Marie chattered incessantly about everything, and Charlotte listened and answered the child's questions. They got on well, had done so from the beginning, but Charlotte couldn't help wondering if the situation might change when they were in France. One thing, she would soon know.

Then Marie dozed, and Yves spoke for the first time since getting in the car. He drove swiftly but very well, not aggressively as so many drivers of large cars did, but with consideration for other road users – although they passed everything within sight on the motorway, Charlotte didn't feel the slightest bit uneasy. She was completely relaxed.

'You will please tell me when you wish to stop for lunch,' he said.

'Yes, of course.' Marie stirred slightly beside her and murmured something in her sleep.

'Good.' After that there was silence again, and Charlotte was left to her own thoughts. She wondered, as she had found herself doing frequently, what Uncle Zhar would be like. She imagined he would be in his thirties. Tall, short, fat or thin? From Marie had come the impression of a tall handsome prince of a man. Charlotte hid a smile. The reality might be completely different. A child's impression of a beloved relative could occasionally colour a picture, and she knew that Marie's imagination was vivid, from other things she had said.

The girl woke soon afterwards, stretched, and yawned, and said: 'I am hungry, Charlotte.'

'You are? Then we'll stop.' She told Yves, and he nodded.

'Very well, miss.'

She thought he would wait until they reached a

motorway restaurant, but he went off at the following turn off, drove a few miles down a country lane, and stopped.

Charlotte looked blankly at him as he turned round. He gave a slight smile, as if sensing her faint alarm. 'Madame Grenier has packed a picnic basket for our lunch,' he told her. 'It is in the boot. Excuse me.'

Silently, efficiently, he unpacked the basket beside the car. They were on a remote country road, and no cars passed. Distantly the motorway throbbed with life, and from a nearby field several cows watched them with complete disdain.

He folded down trays from the back of the front seats, and produced plates. Charlotte thought: I should have known! There was chicken, and ham, salad and fruit, and two thermos jugs of coffee. Paper plates and serviettes and plastic beakers that looked like china. After they had eaten the two girls went for a short walk leaving Yves by the car. A distant farmhouse reminded Charlotte, with a pang, of her own home, and she turned away quickly. 'Come on, Marie, we'll go back now,' she said.

'Yves looks after us well, doesn't he?'

Charlotte smiled. 'Indeed he does. Do you know where we are staying tonight?'

The girl shrugged. 'With friends, I think. Yves has it all written down. Grand'mère is very careful. She gives him all the instructions, and he always does everything right.'

'I'm sure he does.' So they were staying with friends of Madame Grenier in London. Yves would find the place without any trouble, she felt quite sure of that. There was something rather intimidating about such efficiency. Charlotte wondered if the vineyard was run

37

equally well. And that, she thought, as they returned to the car, is something else I shall soon find out. And despite herself, a strange little prickle of excitement ran up her spine.

CHAPTER THREE

CHARLOTTE fought against it, but the thoughts and images of Jared were too powerful to resist, and she stood at the window of the luxurious apartment and let the pictures come. Marie was in bed, fast asleep, Yves was in the kitchen talking to the housekeeper and her husband, and Charlotte was in her bedroom. In the bathroom she shared with Marie a scented bath awaited her, and she was clad only in her dark blue dressing gown, and in a minute she would slide into the pink foaming water and wash all the travel stains away. But now was a quiet moment, a precious few minutes of peace after many miles of travel, and Charlotte stood there in the shadowy room and looked down to the glittering lights of Paris, and remembered.

The traffic along the Champs-Elysées was a muted roar, a rich blur of yellow light, dazzling to the eyes, and Paris hummed with life as it always did at night, and she wondered if Jared was out there in the crowd, sitting perhaps at a table in a restaurant, with some woman . . .

'Stop it!' she told herself. It didn't matter any more. It was all over, had never really begun, and this return visit to Paris might be all she needed to cure her once and for all. Perhaps . . .

'Oh, Jared,' she whispered, putting her forehead to the cool glass. Useless to try and forget the man who had changed her life so suddenly and wonderfully two years ago. She would never forget him. With a quick shrug she turned away from the window. A bath would do her good. Tomorrow they would reach the vineyard, and then there would be no time to think wistfully of a man who couldn't even say good-bye, who had run away . . .

Breakfast was eaten with Marie sitting impishly crosslegged at the foot of her bed. Charlotte spread apricot jam over the meltingly flaky croissant and grinned at her young charge. 'You want some?' she asked.

'Please,' Marie nodded. 'They are delicious. I have had four already.'

'You'll get fat,' Charlotte told her severely.

'Ah, not me,' Marie shook her head. 'Uncle Zhar tells me I will grow up as slender as a gazelle.'

'Hmm, perhaps he's not seen you eating, like I have.'

Marie laughed, full of amusement. 'He has taken me for meals sometimes,' she answered. 'Just the two of us, and occasionally with friends of his. I like *that*.'

'I suppose,' Charlotte said, very casually, 'Uncle Zhar will be there when we arrive at the vineyard today?'

Marie shrugged, too busily engaged in keeping apricot jam off her chin to notice anything in Charlotte's tone. 'He is lovely, my uncle, but he is a strange one too. He goes off sometimes. But I think,' she added thoughtfully, 'I *think* he may be there. I have a little present for him.'

'Ah, then I'm sure he will be,' Charlotte said, smiling. 'Is it a secret, or can you tell me?'

'I will show you,' the girl slid off the bed and ran across to her own adjoining bedroom. A tie? A book?

'There,' a box was being opened carefully and Charlotte peeped in to see a pair of silver cuff-links nestling on a bed of deep velvet. She smiled.

'Why, Marie, I'm sure he'll love those,' she said, and saw the pink spread in the girl's cheeks.

'You think so? Good. It is so difficult to choose presents for a man,' she added with grown-up wisdom. 'For ladies you can buy perfume and make up and lots of nice things, but for a man,' she sighed, 'it is very hard.'

'I know,' Charlotte smiled. She looked at her watch. 'It's nearly nine. I think we'd better get dressed and ready, don't you? Yves will be waiting for us.'

'All right,' Marie obediently took her box back. 'I'll put this away, and have a wash – or do you wish to wash first?'

'No, after you.' Charlotte put her breakfast tray on the table and slid under silk sheets again. She had not slept well, and a few more minutes would be very welcome ...

'Charlotte, come, you have fallen to sleep,' Marie was tapping her arm, and she jerked awake guiltily.

The girl was dressed, her hair brushed dark and shiny, her dress clean and neat.

'Oh, Marie! Heavens – all right, I'll not be a minute.' She scrambled out of bed and flew into the bathroom.

Paris was left behind them, and the road they travelled now was long and straight and wide, lined with tall trees. Marie wasn't tired, although they had been driving for four hours. She sat up, looking eagerly round at the countryside surrounding them.

'Here is my home,' she said proudly. 'The most beautiful country in the world – at least I think so,' and she looked swiftly at Charlotte sitting beside her, who laughed.

'Of course, that is right you should think so, Marie,' she answered. 'Just as I love England, and especially my own county, Yorkshire. And I'll tell you a little secret. I'm looking forward very much to seeing your home too.'

'You will like it, I know.' The girl nodded wisely. 'And my dogs – and the cats. Oh, I have so much to show you.'

Charlotte sat back, and at that moment Yves spoke. 'You wish to stop for a drink?' he asked. 'There is a good café in a few kilometres.'

Charlotte looked at Marie, who nodded. 'Yes, please, Yves,' she answered. It would be a good opportunity to freshen up, nearing the end of their journey.

They sipped ice-cold *sirops* in the garden of the café, just a few yards from the busy main road. Cars of all nationalities were parked at the front, and brightly dressed tourists walked round the garden buying souvenirs from the packed stall behind where they sat. The sun shone down from a cloudless sky, and for no reason Charlotte thought suddenly of Jared, and it was like a pain. Where was he now? Because this was the country where she had met him, the only place she had known him, and yet he had been a wanderer, and he could be anywhere in the world. Anywhere . . .

'I'm sorry, Marie, what did you say?'

'That man looks like Uncle Zhar,' and Marie pointed. Several men were buying gifts at the stall, but Charlotte saw immediately which one Marie had indicated. Of medium height, he was dark and pleasant-looking, and a little boy held his hand tightly. There were other men there, of course, but it was quite obvious that Marie meant the one Charlotte saw, for she could just imagine Uncle Zhar like that.

'Well, you'll soon see him again, won't you?' she said, and turned away, and back to the table. There had been a tall dark figure to one side of the stall, and she would be imagining she was seeing Jared if she wasn't careful, and she must stop *that* at once. The sooner she could put him completely out of her mind, the better.

They ate a light lunch at the café after all, because there were several more hours' travelling to be done, and Yves had assured them that the proprietor was famous for his *omelettes aux fines herbes*. And rightly so. The meal was just enough to satisfy them without filling them, and they set off again refreshed and fed.

The heat grew more intense as they went south. So strong that at times the road ahead shimmered and danced in a kind of mirage. Villages were passed in a blur of grey stone buildings, and colourful dresses, and bright cars, and dogs which darted out as though asking to be run over, and pigeons which flew in front of them as they went more slowly through cobbled streets.

They brought some fruit at another roadside café and sat in the car after drinking iced lemonade, and peeled oranges and bit deep into luscious peaches. Yves was courteous and attentive, never a word out of place, and Marie chattered to him in French, and Charlotte sat there and let it all wash over her. The memory of the man she had glimpsed at their previous stop came back to her, but she determinedly put the image out of her mind lest it disturb her too much. She was going to forget Jared. And the sooner she did so, the better.

Yves phoned to Madame Grenier before they left, to let her know when they would be arriving. So it would not be long now. A small excitement was building up inside Charlotte, and Marie had a rosy flush to her cheeks that told of her own anticipation. Only Yves remained calm, which was just as well, Charlotte reflected, as he was driving.

The road was eaten up smoothly beneath the wheels and the golden day gradually turned to blue dusk, and they passed through yet another village and Marie leaned and touched Charlotte's arm.

43

'We are almost home,' she said. 'We are nearly there.'

Charlotte looked down at her, and smiled. 'And you are tired,' she told her.

'Huh, a little, that is all.'

The stars were out in a deep velvet sky, and the air was fresh and cold, and Charlotte waited. There was a long high wall that seemed to go for miles at the side of the road, and then Yves was slowing the car, and she saw high wrought iron gates swinging slowly open as he turned to go through them. So this was it!

The drive was long and straight and seemingly endless. Then they turned to the right again, and the trees that had hidden the house from view were left behind them, and Charlotte saw her new home for the very first time. Only it wasn't a house. It was a castle, a magnificent high towering white *château*. Nobody had told her that.

The car rolled to a stop, and Yves came round to open the door for them. Both girls got out and Marie ran towards the steps to where a familiar figure waited. Charlotte remained where she was, stunned at the sheer beauty of the building that rose before her, like something out of a fairy tale, ablaze with light from the tall elegant windows and wide doorway.

'Welcome to La Grande Baronnie,' said Madame Grenier as she walked slowly down the steps. 'It is perhaps a surprise to you, *mademoiselle?*'

'A great surprise, *madame*,' agreed Charlotte, going forward to greet her and shake hands. 'It is a beautiful castle. I didn't realize—'

'No? You will see it better by morning, of course. Come in. You have had a good journey?'

'Very good, thank you.' They were going up the grey stone steps, and into a wide hall that shimmered with

44

light and colour. Charlotte blinked, too dazzled to take it in yet. And very tired.

'Come, I have some supper prepared, and then I think it will be time for Marie to go to bed,' and her grandmother ruffled the child's hair fondly.

'But Uncle Zhar – where is he?' Marie asked.

'Ah, *ma petite*, he will be here tomorrow. You will see him in the morning.'

The girl's face fell; although she tried to hide it, she was clearly disappointed.

'He says he is sorry not to be here to greet you, but he had to go to Lyon on urgent business.'

They sat down in a room that had a curved ceiling. The walls were completely white, and covered with tapestries. In the window alcoves, also curved, were murals of brightly coloured battle scenes. Everything about the room was rich, too much for Charlotte's tired eyes to take in – and yet – there had been something strange the moment she had entered, something in the atmosphere of the place. It was almost as if she had been there before, as if she too had come home. A most odd sensation, and one that she put down to travel tiredness, but it returned to haunt her later as she lay at last in a soft comfortable bed in her new bedroom.

The images were bright in her mind, and she lay on her back and let them all wash over her in a multi-coloured kaleidoscope that was almost disturbing in its vividness. And yet out of all the dazzling confusion there came again the sensation she had known when she had first entered the magnificent salon with its curving ceiling. She shivered, for the feeling was almost an eerie one. She had never been here before in her life – and yet there it had been, an instant atmosphere that had reached out to enfold her and touch her with a kind of warmth. It was as if she had known all her life that she was one day to come here. In the last few drowsy minutes before she fell into a deep sleep the words of a poem came into her mind. 'I have been here before, but when or how I cannot tell . . .' She wondered if she would remember who had written those lines. And then she slept.

Nobody came to wake Charlotte in the morning. When she opened her eyes it was to find sunshine streaming in through the two high narrow windows, and a faint breeze stirring the deep gold curtains. She sat up slowly, stretching, and remembered where she was. A clock ticked busily away on the mantelpiece and it said, unbelievably, ten o'clock.

There was no sound. She might have been alone in the world, yet there was nothing worrying in that thought. Charlotte got out of bed and went into the adjoining bathroom, one which she was to share with Marie. She opened the door at the other side and saw the child still fast asleep in a four-poster bed similar to her own. She smiled and softly closed the communicating door. No doubt Madame Grenier had peeped in on her granddaughter and decided to let them both sleep off the effects of their long journey.

She washed and dressed in a simple white dress, one of four that she and Aunt Emily had chosen and bought after the interview in York. And that reminded her that she must write or phone as soon as possible to let her aunt know of their safe arrival. Charlotte brushed her short wavy hair, applied a dash of lipstick, and picking up her handbag, went quietly to her bedroom door and opened it.

There was a faint scent of lavender in the corridor outside. Her feet made no sound on the thick red carpet as she walked quickly downstairs. In the hall, sunlight streamed in through the windows and wide open front door. And her employer appeared as if by magic from the doorway of the beautiful salon, and said:

'Good morning, Charlotte. I may call you Charlotte, I trust?' She acknowledged Charlotte's smiling nod with her own slightly more austere movement of the head. '*Bien*! And did you sleep well?'

'Very well, thank you, *madame*. I had a look at Marie, but she was still fast asleep.'

'Ah yes, I am leaving her until she wakes up. Travelling is very tiring, is it not? Come, I will show you where you will breakfast, and afterwards you must feel free to wander round and find your bearings.'

Charlotte followed the older woman into another larger room across the hall. The magnificence of it took her breath away. High wood-panelled ceiling, with crests and shields pictured in triangles at intervals, it was an imposing room, far grander than the one of the previous night – and yet without that other's warmth.

The long table shone with loving polishing, and french windows were flung wide open, at least six of the them all down one side of the room, all with rich gold curtaining, all admitting the strong sunlight.

'This, as you can see, is the dining room,' Madame Grenier allowed herself a little smile at the obvious wonder on Charlotte's face. 'I see too that you appreciate beauty.'

'The whole castle is quite beyond anything I imagined,' Charlotte answered truthfully.

'I can understand that it might have that effect on anyone when they first arrive, yes,' the older woman agreed. 'But you must not let yourself be – what is the word – overawed by it. It is a home as well as being a beautiful building. I want you to be happy here.'

'Thank you.' The table had two places set at the near

end, and the older woman indicated that Charlotte should sit at one. She seated herself after pressing a bell by the fireplace. 'I will have coffee with you, I think. And then I will show you round the castle.'

The maid who brought in the tray was clearly curious. A pretty dark-haired girl in her late teens, she gave Charlotte several sidelong glances and a quick shy smile as she set out the plate of flaky croissants in front of her.

'*Et café pour moi aussi,* Mado,' said Madame Grenier, as the girl turned to leave.

'*Très bien, madame,*' answered the girl, with a quick bob in the old woman's direction.

Madame Grenier drank her coffee while Charlotte ate her breakfast, and told her briefly about the castle, its age, and some of the history of the family. And at the close of the meal, the old woman said, 'My nephew may return home today. He will probably phone first.'

That reminded Charlotte, and she asked if she could phone very briefly to tell her aunt that all was well.

'Of course. I will take you to the telephone afterwards. But I have already informed your aunt of your safe arrival last night when you and Marie went up to bed.'

'That's very thoughtful of you, *madame,*' Charlotte hid her surprise as best she could, but Madame Grenier smiled.

'Do not be so startled, Charlotte. It was natural for her to be worried. *Eh bien,* I have reassured her. But I'm sure she will be even more pleased to hear your voice.'

'I shall only make it a brief call. I'll write and tell her all about it this evening.'

'And have you any other friends you must write to?'

Charlotte shook her head, cheeks faintly pink. 'Not

48

really. I never had time to make many while I was on the farm. I kept in touch with one or two school friends for a while, of course, but—' she shrugged.

The older woman's face softened slightly. 'That is why I feel you will understand Marie better than most. Her life is of necessity rather lonely, but—' she raised her hand in a Gallic gesture of dismissal, 'that is life, is it not?'

'I feel as if I do understand Marie, *madame*,' Charlotte answered quietly.

'And I think we will get on well while I am here.'

'I am quite sure you will. Well, if we are finished, shall we go?'

The chateau was large, as was obvious from the outside, and the rooms had all been decorated and furnished with great care so as to retain the flavour of the past which was so redolent. The old woman took her time, clearly deriving great pleasure from showing Charlotte round the beautiful building.

There was a library full not only of books, but with cases of exquisite china ornaments and statuettes, a grand piano in the corner, several musical instruments carefully placed, obviously very old, and one very new-looking guitar hanging on the white plaster-washed wall over the fireplace. Charlotte looked from it to her employer, who smiled.

'Ah yes, my nephew's. Marie is also learning it. You must get her to play for you. She does very well.'

'I should like that. And your nephew, Monsieur de Marais – does he play well?'

'I don't know,' was the rather surprising answer. It was accompanied by a faint dismissive shrug. 'My nephew entertains his friends, of course, but I generally find an excuse to go to bed early on those evenings.' Nothing in the words, but a small question was put unwillingly into Charlotte's mind. If there was tension, however slight, in the relationship between Madame Grenier and her nephew, it could make things difficult for Marie. And Charlotte might be able to help there, however slightly. She was already feeling protective towards her new charge. She was also wondering just what this mysterious nephew would be like. The mental picture of Uncle Zhar – a strange name – was clear but could be highly inaccurate. Yet every little thing she heard about him added to the portrait. Maybe he and his aunt were the best of friends. Maybe she was just jumping to conclusions. Maybe . . .

She phoned Aunt Emily very briefly, and promised to write that evening. Marie was up and dressed by this time, and they had a light lunch, after which both girls went to see round the estate, Marie clearly looking forward to showing Charlotte her home – and her animals.

The vines stretched for ever – or so it seemed to Charlotte's bemused eyes. Neat rows and rows and rows of rich dark grapes ripening in the blazing sunlight, and in the distance faint blue hills. So beautiful, yet so completely unlike anything Charlotte had seen before.

Two labradors appeared from nowhere and bounded up barking excitedly to greet them, Marie with love, Charlotte with slight reservations until Marie introduced her as a friend. They were huge golden dogs, well groomed and cared for, and they followed obediently as the two walked on away from the castle. Charlotte looked back and drew in her breath at the sheer beauty and majesty of it, as she gazed at the white turrets, dazzling in the sun, the clock set in one tower, the long high windows, many open, others tightly shut. She had seen most of the castle that morning after breakfast, yet it was impossible to take in its sheer grandeur or atmosphere in such a brief look round. There would be other times, with Marie, to do so.

Behind the castle, to the right of it were many long low outbuildings. Charlotte pointed to them and asked Marie what they were for.

'Oh, I will show you. Come.' It was a relief to get out of the sun, for in the middle of the afternoon, and with not a single cloud in the sky to hide it for even a moment, the heat was intense.

It took her eyes several seconds to adjust to the gloom of that first shadowy building, and Charlotte hesitated by the door blinking. Rows and rows of barrels stood silently like sentinels, and seeming to stretch as endlessly as the vines themselves did outside.

Marie laughed and pulled Charlotte's arm. 'Come, this is dull,' she said, 'come and see the horses.'

The stables were further along. High hedges blocked their view of the château and it was very English, approaching those familiar doors, open at the top, to see horses' heads looking out, curious to know who the visitors were.

'Why, Marie, you never mentioned horses,' said Charlotte. 'Do you ride?'

The girl pulled a face. 'Only when Uncle Zhar is here – unless—' she took a deep breath and her eyes widened. 'Can you – do *you*—?'

'Of course! Do you think your grandmother would let me take you out?' Marie jumped up and hugged Charlotte before she could finish the sentence. Her eyes lit with sheer happiness as she called out:

'I will go and ask her *now*. Oh, Charlotte—' and then she was gone, running swiftly before Charlotte could stop her or tell her to wait. The dogs ran after her barking excitedly because something was happening, even if they didn't know what it was.

Charlótte turned back to the first velvet-eyed horse and put out her hand. 'Hello, boy,' she said.

She walked to the second door and spoke to a bright-eyed animal that shied away and snorted. The third door was wide open, both sections of it, and as she neared it a man came out and then turned towards her as if realizing suddenly that he was not alone.

A big man, dressed in jeans and denim top, and with espadrilles on his feet. Charlotte jerked to a standstill, her head going back in stunned disbelief. The memories of Jared were still painful, but she didn't think she was so bad that she was now going to start seeing him everywhere.

Her hand went to her mouth to hide the pain. And then he spoke, and his voice was flat, harsh, equally disbelieving.

'What are you doing here?' he said.

CHAPTER FOUR

FOR a moment Charlotte didn't speak. She couldn't. She felt, terrifyingly, as if she were going to faint, but it passed, and she found her voice.

'Jared,' she said. 'It is you.'

He came nearer. His face was precisely as she remembered from so many painful dreams. Yet gone was the tenderness, the love with which he had once looked at her. Those tawny gold eyes were hard now, like a stranger's.

'Why are you here?' he repeated. 'Who sent you?'

Swift flaring anger replaced her astonishment. She looked up at him, eyes lit with a quick rare temper. If he thought she had come chasing after him, he would soon discover just how mistaken he was.

'I work here,' she said quickly. 'No one *sent* me. And what are *you* doing here? Don't tell me you work here too—' she caught her breath. It was like one of those dreams that suddenly turn into a nightmare. That she should be talking to him like this was bad enough – almost unimaginable – but even worse was his own attitude as he stood there before her, tall, powerful – seemingly angry. Angry? Jared? She had never known him like this in those few blissful days in Paris.

And then he laughed. There was no real humour in it, none at all.

'Ah, come on,' he said. 'Don't give me that. You've—' he stopped, because there was a scurry of flying footsteps, and Marie's excited shout:

'Uncle Zhar! Grand'mère *m'a dit*—'

Uncle Zhar. Zhar – Jared. Waves of horrified real-

53

ization swept over Charlotte in that stunned instant of time. A girl's pet nickname for her uncle, and she had not even for a moment connected the two names.

Marie flung herself in Jared's arms, to be swept upwards, and Charlotte heard him say, in French, 'So you're back are you, little one? And what have you been doing, hey?'

It gave her time to recover slightly. She fought desperately to hide the trembling shock she still felt. Time to think when she was alone. The important thing now was not to let him – not to let this hostile *stranger* – see just what effect he had had on her.

Marie turned, her face alight with happiness. 'This is Charlotte,' she said, speaking in English as if remembering. 'She has come from England to look after me. Charlotte, this is my Uncle Zhar.'

Charlotte nodded, smiled, but didn't offer her hand. 'I'm pleased to meet you,' she said. She met his eyes now. She could manage that. 'Marie has told me a lot about you.'

Something touched his face, a fleeting expression, then it was gone.

'I'm delighted to meet you – Charlotte,' he said. 'I trust Marie is showing you round?'

'Oh yes,' Marie answered before Charlotte could do so. 'Grand'mère says I may go riding with her tomorrow – I forgot you would be home, though.' She wrinkled her nose thoughtfully. 'Perhaps we can all go together? Yes?' She looked up at her uncle anxiously.

Jared laughed. 'We'll see.' His eyes met Charlotte's. There was a warning in them, a warning to her not to say anything. She lifted her chin. She had no intention of doing so. Let him speak. Let her hear what he had to say. For there was something seriously amiss here, and she wanted to know what it was.

But the time to discover what was not going to be now. Jared turned away towards the open stable door. 'Come, Prince,' he said. A magnificent bay stallion emerged, throwing his head back in anticipation, ready saddled.

'*Au revoir*, ladies,' Jared said, with only a faint tinge of what could have been mockery in his voice.

'But, Uncle—'

'Later, Marie. I will see you later.' The big man mounted the horse, and the picture they made caused Charlotte's heart to quicken. Two truly magnificent-looking animals – she had never pictured Jared riding, but he looked so right. He looked down on them, and the hostility she had seen was now veiled. Then he nodded, and they trotted away towards the drive, and when the echoing hooves had vanished, there was nothing.

Perhaps it had all been a bad dream, thought Charlotte. She still shook inwardly with shock, but Marie noticed nothing of this.

'My grandmother told me that Uncle Zhar had returned,' she said excitedly, 'when I went to ask her about riding. How *nice* that you should meet. I am so pleased. Do you not think he is lovely?'

'He seems very – pleasant.' Charlotte hesitated only slightly, for how did you begin to tell anyone what had just happened, who he *really* was? You didn't.

'Yes. Come, we will return to the house. There are drinks waiting for us – it is such a hot afternoon. I am surprised Uncle Zhar should want to go out riding in this heat. But then—' she gave a graceful, almost womanly shrug, 'men are funny, are they not?'

Funny isn't the word I'd use, thought Charlotte. Not about him. Her head began to ache, and she wanted to be alone, just to think about the situation, but she was

55

going to have to act as if everything were normal. She didn't realize how difficult that would be – nor how shrewd Madame Grenier was.

As they entered the long cool room in which Charlotte had received such a distinct impression of *déjà vu* – of having been there before – the previous night, the older woman looked up and frowned slightly.

'Why, Charlotte, you are quite pale,' she said. 'Come and sit down. Marie should not have kept you out so long in the heat.'

Before Charlotte could answer, Marie spoke. 'We met Uncle Zhar,' she said, smiling. 'He is going out riding.'

'Ah yes, he returned after lunch.' The old woman nodded, and her keen dark eyes were on Charlotte, who sat down gratefully on an elegant brocade-covered settee. Marie passed her a long cool drink and she sipped at the icy fruit syrup wondering if there was anything in her face to give her away.

'So, you have met Jared—' she too pronounced it in a similar way to her granddaughter, more like Zhard, 'at last. He insisted on going out on Prince straightaway.' She smiled slightly. 'I sometimes think he is more fond of horses than of humans.' Then as if regretting an indiscretion, 'But that is life, is it not? Who knows, perhaps he is right?' But her eyes were suddenly darker – almost cold.

There was nothing Charlotte could say, and she had no desire to talk about the man who had come into her life so abruptly – so shockingly – again. 'This drink is delicious, *madame*,' she remarked. 'And I enjoyed seeing round the vineyards. I didn't image they would be so enormous.'

'Ah no?' She shrugged. 'They have been in the family for generations. I was born here. I moved away when I married but returned on the death of my brother Gilles, when the vineyard passed into the hands of my son Paul, and Gilles' son Jared.'

'I see.' Charlotte had no desire to hear family secrets, but it seemed that Madame Grenier was disposed to talk, and there seemed no harm in one small question anyway. 'Then Marie and J – Monsieur de Marais are second cousins?'

'Yes. But as he is so much older she has always known him as uncle.'

'Of course,' Charlotte smiled. There was another question, but how dared she ask it? Perhaps Madame Grenier was a mind-reader, for the next moment she said:

'Did you not find it strange that my nephew spoke such good English?'

'I – I – had wondered, yes.' But then, two years ago, I had thought him to be an American – certainly not a Frenchman, Charlotte added silently.

'His mother is American. She took him all over the world when he was younger, instead of settling him to his heritage—' she stopped abruptly, because Marie was listening intently. '*Tiens*, child, you have Mademoiselle Lucy here for lessons tomorrow. Go and prepare your books.'

'But you said I could go out with Charlotte riding, Grand'mère.' Obediently the girl left the room, and Madame Grenier sighed. 'Ah, you will get no peace now. I should have warned you, Charlotte. Marie is obsessed with horses as well.'

Charlotte laughed, partly with relief at the change of subject. 'That's fine by me, *madame*,' she answered. 'I love horses too. It was a surprise to see them here, and they are beautiful animals. It will be a pleasure to ride. Are we allowed to go anywhere?'

57

'Well,' the old lady frowned thoughtfully, 'my nephew will be the best one to advise you on that subject. There is good riding country hereabouts, and one is perfectly safe. You will have a talk with him this evening.'

It all came back to Charlotte in a sudden wash of panic – the memory of Jared's face when he had greeted her outside the stables. He not only didn't want to talk to her, she felt sure, he didn't want her there. But why? What reason could there be for the startling hostility? She possessed the quality of patience. She would wait. After all, she reflected, she had no choice anyway.

There was something she wanted to know, and as it seemed quite reasonable to ask, she said: '*Madame*, where shall I eat? With Marie?'

The old woman seemed mildly surprised. 'Why, Marie eats with Jared and me. As you will too.' She hesitated. 'There will be occasions, naturally, when we entertain guests – you understand – when Marie has her evening meal in the nursery adjoining her room, then of course—' she paused.

'Of course, *madame*.' She tried to hide the dismay. To have to eat with *him*! Perhaps he would put a stop to it, she thought. For he was the man in charge, no doubt about that. She bit her lip. It would be humiliating, but in one way it would be a relief. For the thought of having to make polite conversation with him while she tried to eat was an impossible one. She would just wait and see.

But Jared was not there at dinner that evening. For the hour beforehand Charlotte wrote to Aunt Emily in her room, and it was difficult to make the letter lighthearted, hard not to blurt out the truth on paper. Instead she described the *château*, the extensive vineyards, the

58

horses – and not a word of Jared. For how did you tell anyone what had happened? Her aunt had met him briefly on that Parisian holiday, and liked him. But he had never been mentioned since. And her aunt was so delighted that the post she had chosen, had had a 'feeling' about, had turned out so very right that Charlotte would not even have known how to begin.

She finished the letter with a sigh of relief. The next one would be easier to write, she felt sure as she sealed the envelope and addressed it. Putting in on the dresser in her bedroom, she picked up her handbag and went downstairs, filled with trepidation.

A deep gong sounded as she reached the hall, and she crossed to the large dining-room to see Madame Grenier and Marie already seated waiting.

'Good. Sit down, Charlotte.' There were only the three places set at the end of the long dining table. 'My nephew has had to go out again, so we will begin.' She nodded, presumably to some servant waiting by the door, for Charlotte heard quick footsteps moving away.

She made a mental note, as each course was served, to write to Aunt Emily with all details. She would appreciate that, with her interest in food and wine. And although it was delicious, right down to the fresh peaches which served in place of any other sweet, Charlotte had little appetite, and had to force herself to eat.

Marie went to bed after the meal, and Charlotte and her employer went into what she now privately thought of as her room – the main lounge of the castle. Seated there, Madame Grenier said: 'Now that your day is over, Charlotte, I will tell you that your evenings are free to do as you wish. There is, alas, not much entertainment for you outside the château. The nearby village is small, with only one cinema – a place I do not recommend. But we have television, and you are free to watch that. Also the library – take what books you wish to read. At weekends Yves will take you and Marie out in the car for rides, perhaps for picnics.'

'Thank you, *madame*,' Charlotte smiled, aware of the older woman's concern. 'I'll be quite happy with books in the evenings. I'm not used to going out at night anyway. And of course I'll enjoy watching television sometimes. Do you ever watch?'

'Ah, sometimes. I am an old woman. Bed at ten o'clock for me, I'm afraid.'

Charlotte nodded. 'Not only you. I had to get up early on the farm, so I'm usually in bed by then. If I may take a book up tonight—' she hesitated.

'*Mais naturellement!* Go now if you wish. I will sit here until you return. I find this room very restful.'

Suddenly it seemed the most natural thing in the world to tell the old woman about her own feelings on first entering it. She didn't know why but as she stood up to go out to the library, Charlotte said: 'I had the strangest sensation when I came in here for the first time. It was as if I had been here before—' and she stopped, biting her lip, wondering if her words sounded foolish to the other's ears.

There was an odd expression on the old woman's face. She nodded, her eyes dark as she looked up at Charlotte. 'Yes, yes. I was not mistaken – I saw something on your face when you came in. I was watching. How strange, Charlotte, that you should feel that. How very strange.' There was something in her words that made Charlotte stop, and the old woman went on: 'Like all old buildings – and this is very old, as I'm sure you can imagine – there is an atmosphere that has come down through the years. I don't mean ghosts, or anything like that, but a certain *esprit* – a spirit to the place.

60

And this room has always been a happy one for me.' She stopped and shook her head gently, sighing.

'It is where I first met my dear late husband.' Charlotte could not be sure, but it seemed as if tears might gleam in those dark eyes. She would not have interrupted the old woman for the world. 'And where he proposed to me. Yes, it holds many memories for me – but how strange that you too should feel this when you entered it. You must be very sensitive.'

Charlotte smiled. 'I don't know. I just felt I had to tell you, though.'

'Yes, yes. I am pleased that you did. These things happen. Who knows why? We do not understand everything – and it is as well that we do not. Ah well, away with you, child, to find your book. Then return to me here.'

'Yes, *madame*.' And Charlotte went quietly out to the library. The powerful lights in the chandeliers flooded the room with gold when she pressed the switch by the door. She stood for a moment to get her bearings before moving towards the first rows of books. The choice was overwhelming. Books in both English and French. New ones, old ones, thick and thin ones, the shelves were crammed with richness enough for the greediest bookworm. She moved along the shelves, pausing, taking one out for a moment, constantly amazed at the variety of literature thereon. Charlotte had vaguely imagined that the library would be old-fashioned, the books heavy in both weight and content, but she was wrong. The whole series of James Bond thrillers sat next to another set – in English – on Hollywood Movies through the Years. There were books on vine-growing, diseases in vineyards – these in French – the complete Encyclopaedia Britannica – short stories by Somerset Maugham next to those of Guy de Maupassant.

Charlotte took a deep breath and eventually picked a volume of poems and a detective novel by Margery Allingham. She switched off the lights before leaving the room, and went back to join her employer.

She tried to read, to shut out the disturbing thoughts of Jared, but it was in vain. Putting the novel to one side, she gave herself up to the memories of what had happened only hours previously, lying back on her pillow looking at a shaft of moonlight as it slanted across the ceiling. Cool grey-yellow, the light was restful, but she did not see it. She saw a man's face instead, a hostile, unwelcoming face. Jared. There had been, she knew now, the faint idea at the back of her mind that one day she would meet him again. Impossible to deny even to herself, but she could never have imagined such a setting for their meeting.

Charlotte closed her eyes. How much better it would have been had Aunt Emily not seen that advertisement in the paper. No – Charlotte frowned. Not true. For she had a genuine affection for Marie, and the desire to help this lonely child, and she knew the affection was returned. Together they would speak English, go riding, share the discoveries to be made in books, and Charlotte would justify her employment by Madame Grenier – and she would learn to harden her heart about Jared so that it would not matter – *he* would not matter.

She turned her head restlessly on the pillow. It was easy to tell it to herself. Simple to decide, but maybe not so easily done. But there was one thing she was determined, which she had a right to know, and that was to hear why, from Jared himself, he was so hostile. And then she would try to put him out of the place he had so long unknowingly occupied in her heart. She suddenly felt very tired. With the making of the decision, the restlessness left her. Charlotte closed her eyes. A few minutes later she was asleep.

A noise woke her up hours later and she sat up, wondering if at first it was Marie – then realized that the sound was a car door closing. She ran barefooted to the window and looked out. The moon had vanished behind a cloud, everything was dark and shadowy, but there was no mistaking the figure walking away from the long sleek sports car standing outside. So Jared had come home.

Charlotte crept back to bed and picked up the clock from her little table. The luminous dial told her that it was four-thirty. She wondered where Jared had been. But there was no one to tell her. It took her longer to get to sleep that second time.

Marie was occupied with her lessons, Madame Grenier had gone out with Yves in the Daimler, and Charlotte went into the library because she had nothing to do for an hour until Marie was finished. She imagined that Jared would still be in bed. Already she had begun the painful process of hardening her heart against him. She bent to a bottom shelf where she had seen some promising-looking books the previous night, and turned as there came a faint sound from the doorway, and Jared walked in.

Charlotte stood up slowly, her heart threatening to burst with the shock. She tried to keep her face calm – and she looked at him.

'Charlotte,' he said, and came over to her. She waited silently. Let him speak.

'I thought I would find you here,' he said.

'Did you? Why?' It was an effort to speak calmly, but she managed it because something told her it was important to do so.

He looked down at her. Impossible to tell what was in his eyes this morning. He looked tired, but then, she thought, he would be with only a few hours' sleep.

'It's the most interesting room in the house, that's why.'

'Is it? I came because I like books, and Marie is having her lessons.' Then she turned to face him fully. One hand on a library shelf kept her steady. 'Why were you so rude to me yesterday?' There, it was said. She felt almost lightheaded.

'Don't you *know?*' he said, and was like a stranger speaking.

'I wouldn't ask if I did,' she answered, surprised at how much easier it became with each minute that passed.

He looked at her for a moment. How tall, how strong he looked – and yet how different from that carefree man of two years ago. Then he spoke, and the new hardness of his eyes was matched by his voice. 'You're either a very good actress or a natural liar,' he said. The words were like blows, and she flinched, unable to help herself, then fought for calm.

'Do you think I knew you were here?' she gasped. 'How dare you speak to me like that!'

'I'll speak to you how I like,' he answered swiftly. 'This is my house.'

'And I'm only an employee here – yes, I see.' She couldn't hide the anger in her eyes now, they blazed with it. 'If I had known you were the "Uncle Zhar" Marie spoke about, I wouldn't have come, I promise you that. You made your feelings quite clear two years ago when you sent me those roses with a letter. Do you think I would have come chasing after you or something? My God, but you're conceited!' She turned away, nearly blinded by temper and tears, but managed to say, as she moved: 'I'll get out of *your library*.'

He caught her arm as she passed him. 'Just a moment,' he said. She didn't want him to see the scalding tears. She had to get out. With a strong effort she knocked his hand away.

'Don't *touch* me,' she said loudly. 'You may be the boss here, and I a mere employee – but that doesn't mean you can touch me – ever!'

She swung past him, ran out of the room, and swiftly up the stairs to the safety of her bedroom. With trembling hands she bolted the door and went over to the bed.

Sitting there, recovering from the shock of what had just happened, Charlotte tried to remember what had been said. It wasn't easy at first. She rubbed the place on her arm where his hand had tried to hold her. It burned like fire. What had he called her – either a good actress or a natural liar? So he imagined she had come chasing after him. It was like some nightmare that could only get worse, for whatever she said, he would not believe her. She put her hand to her cheeks, feeling the wetness where tears had been. She would have given anything for him not to have seen them.

It was nearly lunchtime, and before she went down to it she would wash and put some make-up on. It was important for her to look her best. At least she would feel more confident then, and how she needed it! She went to the washbasin by the window and rinsed her face and hands in cool water. Then she sat by the dressing table, and praying that she could remember exactly what Aunt Emily had done, she began to apply make-up, very carefully. The concentration needed had the effect of soothing her somewhat. And as she worked, gently applying a touch of eye-shadow, smoothing it in, she made the effort to see the situation from Jared's point of view. He had a light holiday flirtation with a naïve English girl – that was certainly all it had been for him, she knew that now, and the sooner she accepted the fact, the better it would be.

And then out of the blue, this same stupid English girl had appeared at his home – and denied all knowledge of him. Charlotte closed her eyes for a moment. Of course he didn't believe her. Looking at it logically, as she was now attempting to do, it was hardly to be wondered that his reaction had been the one it had. Yet how could she explain to him? She couldn't. All the talking in the world would not convince him that she hadn't somehow found out who he was, where he lived, and jumped at the chance of a job that would enable her to see him again.

Then she looked at her reflection in the mirror. That was it! Surely Madame Grenier would be able to sort it out in just a few words. The advertisement had been a box number, the interview in an anonymous hotel room where she couldn't possibly have – and then Charlotte stopped, putting down the lipstick she had only just picked up. It was no good. The old woman would wonder at the reason for the explanations – and if she knew that her nephew and Charlotte had met previously, would she not herself begin to ask questions? Charlotte could not bear that. She might be asked to leave, and that was unthinkable now. Marie was learning to trust and accept her as a friend; she was the important one, not Jared. Charlotte picked up the lipstick again, and steadying her hand, began to apply it. Dreadful as the situation was, she had no choice but to accept it. It might even, she thought, be a good thing. Seeing the man as he really was, and not how her memory had coloured him for two long years, would help her to get over him at last. It was almost as though he were two people; the happy-go-lucky wanderer she had known and fallen in love with, and this grim-faced man with his hard eyes and cruel accusations. Only when she reconciled the two would she be cured. And the sooner she managed to do that, the better for her. Her face looked back at her from the mirror. She saw a new calmness, almost an acceptance, in her eyes. She wasn't aware of the soft shining beauty of her features. Only others could see that. Walking slowly, she went to the door and unlocked it, took a deep breath and went down to face Jared at lunch.

CHAPTER FIVE

IT was as if Fate was determined to throw them together. How odd it was, Charlotte reflected after lunch, as she went outside to meet Jared and Marie at the stables. She had stayed behind because Madame Grenier had asked her to do so. It was to impress on Charlotte the fact that she was not to let Marie out of her sight when they were on their ride, and she had assured the older woman that she would be careful on that score.

Stepping out into the heat, she thought back over the lunch, when yet another side of the puzzle that was Jared had been shown. He had been the perfect host, treating her with a cool courtesy that could not have been faulted. And now he was going to choose a horse for her, and one for his niece, because his aunt had asked him to do so. How cleverly he had hidden the resentment he must have felt, for his tone, when he had answered Madame Grenier, had been quite pleasant.

She walked towards the stables, and heard the voices of the two standing there talking, Jared and Marie. There was a third man – Yves. Charlotte had scarcely seen him since their arrival, although she had met most of the other staff, and some of the vineyard workers. Jared turned round at her approach.

'Yves is going with you today,' he said. 'Until you can find your way around.'

'I see.' Charlotte smiled at Yves. 'Hello,' she greeted him.

He bowed very slightly. *'Bonjour, mademoiselle.'* His eyes met and held hers for an instant, and Charlotte was aware that Jared noticed.

'Marie has her own horse, and you may ride Prince today.' Jared's eyes were very cool as they glanced at Charlotte. 'He is a good beast. You are experienced?'

She smiled. 'I've ridden horses since I was five,' she said. 'I've lived on a farm all my life, Monsieur de Marais. I'm sure I'll be able to handle Prince.' There was no flicker of reaction at her formal use of his name, but he turned away and opened the stable door without another word. Charlotte felt strange, as if she was an onlooker watching a scene being enacted in a play. Marie was too excited to notice anything, but Yves looked at Charlotte and gave a slight smile. Dark gipsy eyes held a certain awareness and she caught her breath. Better if he guessed nothing was amiss. She turned to Marie, who like herself had changed into slacks and shirt. The girl's cheeks glowed, and her eyes were alight with anticipation as she returned Charlotte's grin.

'I will take you somewhere very nice,' she said.

'Good. I'm looking forward to this ride,' Charlotte answered. Three horses were ready, beautiful, well groomed animals with glossy coats and alert eyes. One, the smallest, clearly Marie's, whinnied softly and the girl went to him and patted his nose. 'Patience, my little Pierre,' she said. 'Patience.'

Jared lifted her up on to the horse's back. As he did so, Charlotte took Prince's bridle, and talking softly, led him to the mounting block outside the stable door. Even if he had the intention of helping her in the same way as he had his niece, *she* had no intention of letting him. She slid her right leg over and seated herself comfortably, and heard Jared's voice. 'One moment. I will adjust the stirrups.'

She waited, reins in hand, and he bent to alter the straps, and said: 'Is that better?'

She tested them. 'Yes, thank you, *monsieur*.' Cool voice. It was becoming easier than she had expected. She held tightly to the reins, wondering why she should have the sudden almost uncontrollable urge to strike the man. Something perhaps showed in her eyes as she looked down at him, for he glanced up sharply, his own eyes narrowing as he moved away.

Yves sat comfortably on his own mount, and Jared gave a nod. 'All well?'

Marie waved to him. 'Of course. *Au revoir*, Uncle Zhar.'

'*Au revoir*, Marie. Be good.' He returned her salute, and Charlotte looked straight ahead of her, keeping behind Yves the leader, not looking back at all as they set off down the magnificent drive that led to the road. She began to relax once she knew Jared was out of sight. She would not let him spoil her pleasure by thinking about him. There was an hour's good riding ahead of them at least, and it was months since she had been in the saddle, and this was a new, beautiful countryside for her to see.

Yves said something to Marie, and she answered. He nodded, then put his horse ahead again, leaving the two girls to ride side by side. 'He asked where we wanted to go, and I told him,' Marie said.

Charlotte laughed. 'I see. And where is that?'

'It is a surprise.'

'Oh. That's nice.'

It really was too hot to talk, and the horses were content to move at a steady trot along the wide flat drive. It was the first time that Charlotte had been outside the estate since her arrival, which had been in the dark, so that was new to her, and she looked at her surroundings with interested eyes as they went along the road, lined with tall leafy trees that provided some shade from the fierce sun.

Traffic passed, and in the distance she could see the village, but before they reached it they struck off across a field, careful to skirt the edges, for more vines grew there. Charlotte wondered if this too was de Marais property, but did not ask. It did not seem important. Nothing did, save the pleasure of riding a beautiful horse that responded to her every touch, an animal with whom she felt instinctively akin. Then they were climbing, quite gradually, and distant mountains beckoned, cool and unapproachable.

'I have a flask of wine,' said Yves, 'if anyone is thirsty.' She should have known! If I have any more, she thought, I'll fall asleep. One glass with lunch had been sufficient, and that only drunk to steady her nerves in the silent battle with her employer's nephew.

'Not for me, thanks. Not yet, anyway,' she added. It was cooler in the wood they now entered, and thin shafts of sunlight were all that pierced the green shade. Perhaps this was Marie's destination. She waited for the girl to call a halt, but she didn't. They left the wood behind, and she looked back, downwards, and caught her breath at the dizzying splendour of the view. The castle dominated the landscape, a white pearl amidst the rich green of vines and trees. Distant figures moved, as small as ants, and doubtless as busy. And the air shimmered with heat. It was so achingly beautiful that it brought a lump to Charlotte's throat.

The earth was dry underfoot, the horses slowed their pace, and Marie said: 'We are nearly there. Soon – over this hill – you will see why we have come.'

Charlotte waited. It could hardly be more interesting than that which they had left behind. The animals picked their way delicately over rock-strewn ground, and no one spoke, so that the only sound was of hoofs on stone.

They reached the summit of the hill, and there before them was a village with houses and shops, and a fountain in the centre of the one street, and cobblestoned everywhere, and trees shivering their leaves faintly in a slight breeze. They both looked at Charlotte, and she knew why they were watching her, quite suddenly, as she realized what was wrong.

The fountain was silent; no water filled its basin. Nothing moved, save the trees, no person walked that cobbled street, no pigeons flew above it. The town was deserted.

'It's – empty,' she said at last, when she had found her voice.

'It's my ghost village,' said Marie. 'No one lives here any more. Is it not a strange place?'

'Very strange,' agreed Charlotte, and dismounted, followed by Yves, who helped Marie from her horse. He tethered the animals in the shade and returned to them, smiling, looking at Charlotte.

'We'll show Charlotte round,' Marie said to him in French. It was an odd sensation to peep in at open front doors, to see the occasional chair, or bed, threadbare pieces of carpet – and not a soul, not even an animal. An open shutter creaked slightly, and Marie jumped, then laughed.

'I thought it was a ghost!' she exclaimed.

'Why is the village deserted?' Charlotte asked.

'It has been empty for ages. All the wells dried up one year, and the vines died, and people moved away, and those that stayed had to rely on a water cart to bring them fresh water once a week,' Yves answered, speaking in French. He shrugged. 'Soon there were only a few old people left, and gradually, as time passed, they too died, until one day there was just one old woman, Madame le Brun. Her son came and took her away to live with him, and so the village died.'

'But it's like something out of a weird film,' said Charlotte. 'I'm seeing it, but I can't believe it.'

'It happens,' he said. 'That is life. There is nothing here now.'

They sat in the shade of a huge oak tree and he produced the flask of wine from his hip pocket and unscrewed the metal cap which also served as beaker.

Both girls drank enough to quench their thirst and he finished the flask off and put it back. Whether it was the wine or the heat, Charlotte didn't know, but she experienced a feeling almost of lightheadedness. She looked round at the deserted village street, the cracked fountain, its basin now full of dead leaves, and the uncanny stillness of the air, as if time itself stood still here. Then it was time to leave, and they stood up brushing the dust from their clothes and walking slowly back to where the horses were tethered. Something gleamed in a gutter, and Charlotte bent to pick it up. A metal button with an anchor on it, perhaps from a boy's sailor suit or a woman's dress. Maybe it had lain there for years. She put the button in her trouser pocket, not knowing why, except that in some way she wanted a souvenir of their visit to a silent, ghost village.

It grew warmer as they went down the hill again. The lightheadedness had passed, yet there still clung to her a sense of unreality. Almost a feeling that if she were to rush back, the place would have vanished. She chided herself. What an absurd thought! But it was almost a relief to see again the château, and the vines stretching away into the distance, and nearer, cars whizzing along the main road. Here was the real world – and Jared.

Charlotte took a deep breath. She had managed to

forget him for a while. Perhaps he would have gone out. She hoped so.

Yves said something to make her laugh just as they were rounding the outbuildings towards the stables. Marie was well ahead and could not hear, but his remark was a trivial one, only mildly amusing – in fact she forgot it immediately. Some comment about the effect of too much sun and wine, and she threw back her head and laughed, as a relief from a certain tension. Jared was there, watching them, and he saw.

He went over to Marie, who put out her arms to be lifted down. 'You enjoyed your ride, little one?' he asked her. And although he smiled at his niece there was a hardness about his face – and instinctively Charlotte knew that he had been displeased at her laughter. A stab of satisfaction touched her. Good. She must laugh more often with Yves. Though why he should have such a reaction she did not know. She dismounted, as did Yves himself, who said:

'Shall I attend to the horses, *monsieur?*'

'No, Yves, you may go. My aunt wants you.'

'*Merci, monsieur.*' He turned to Charlotte and Marie. '*A votre service, mesdemoiselles.*' He saluted and turned away again to go towards the château. So that was the reason Jared had been waiting for them, thought Charlotte. Because his aunt wanted Yves. Or was it?

She began to lead Prince into his stable, and Jared asked. 'Where are you going?'

'Why, to rub Prince down,' she answered.

'Perhaps you didn't hear me tell Yves that I would attend to them,' he began, but Marie interrupted him: 'Oh no, Uncle Zhar, let us help, please. We would like that, wouldn't we, Charlotte?' Charlotte waited, and looked at Jared – and smiled slightly. Not easy, but she

74

did it, because for some odd reason, just at that moment, she felt supremely confident. It was a pleasant sensation, after the doubts and uncertainties of the past couple of days, and she intended to make the most of it.

'As you wish. Come, let us get these animals out of the heat first,' and he led Yves' mount into the stable, followed by the girls. It was light and airy and clean inside, with the faint scent of hay, and Charlotte looked about her in approval. A comment of Madame Grenier's, that Jared cared more for animals than humans, might well be true, she thought. Perhaps *that* was why he had been so hostile to her. She repressed a giggle at the thought. So engrossed was she in unsaddling Prince that she was hardly aware of Jared addressing her until he repeated the question. 'How did you find Prince?'

'He's a beautiful animal,' she told him with truth. 'I enjoyed riding him very much.'

'We went to the old village,' Marie said, 'and Charlotte was very surprised.'

'Ah yes?' her uncle replied. 'But you must never go there alone, you know that.'

'I can go with Charlotte,' she answered. 'Grand'mère says I can.'

'I prefer you not to.' There was a flat certainty about his tone, and Marie looked sharply at him.

'Why not?' It was the first time that Charlotte had heard her question anything an adult told her. Good for you, she thought.

'Because I say so, that is why.'

'Oh! You are not fair!' And Marie rushed out of the stable. Charlotte busied herself rubbing down Prince, her face straight. If he expected her to comment on the little scene, he was going to be disappointed.

He waited until her running footsteps had died away,

then looked across at Charlotte. Immediately tension filled the air, now that they were alone, and she knew that he was aware of it too.

'Well?' he said.

She paused in her task and met that hard gaze. 'Well what?'

'Have you nothing to say?'

'No. I haven't. It's no business of mine how you deal with your niece. Don't worry, *Monsieur de Marais*,' she accented the words heavily. 'I don't take sides.'

'Good. But I had a reason for being so bossy – as I'm sure you must think I was.'

'Did you? And do you expect me to ask what it was? I'm not going to.'

'I'll tell you anyway. There are occasionally tramps and gipsies who go to the village to camp. Do I need to explain further?'

She hesitated. 'We saw nobody this afternoon.'

'Perhaps not. You were with Yves anyway. He's well able to take care of you.'

'You talk as if we wouldn't be safe.'

'No. And so, I'm telling *you* now, you don't go to the village with Marie again, unless Yves or I am with you.'

She raised her eyebrows in astonishment. '*You*?'

'I often go out riding with Marie, why are you so surprised?'

'Forgive me,' she laughed. 'Did I look surprised? But then it's hardly to be wondered at. I mean, I don't imagine you'd want *me* with you when you take Marie out or not after your enthusiastic reception the other day.' She was being reckless and stupid, she knew that, but she couldn't hold the words back.

She saw quick anger – as quickly controlled as he said: 'As you are employed to be companion to Marie –

that *is* your job, isn't it? – I would naturally expect you to accompany us, and so would my aunt.'

'Yes, of course,' she nodded. 'That *is* what Madame Grenier would expect.'

She turned away, because there was a tightness about his face and she was almost frightened. She didn't want to see it. The fragile bubble of her new-found self-confidence was ready to burst. He must not know.

There were dragging footsteps outside, a pause, then Marie entered. Her eyes went straight to Jared, who looked sharply at her but said nothing.

'I – I'm sorry Uncle Zhar,' she said. Charlotte felt a rush of protectiveness to the little girl. If he spoke harshly to her now, she would have to walk out, she knew. Or she would say something she would surely regret.

Then he smiled. She was watching him as he did so, and her heart gave a quick painful flip. Just like those other smiles, when . . .

'That's all right, Marie.' He rumpled her hair and the child flung her arms round him. 'There were reasons, little one, as I told Charlotte. Sometimes strangers go there to stay for a few days. It is not safe for women alone.'

'Then you will take us, perhaps?'

'I'll see. Don't try and bully me.'

'Pooh! As if I could – as if anyone could bully you.'

'You do your best. Now, attend to Pierre, and then we will go in for a drink of something.'

'Yes, Uncle.' The child obediently bent to her task, and they worked in silence until the horses were comfortable.

It was strange going into her favourite room with him, seeing him sit at ease on the long settee, while Marie sat beside him. Charlotte hesitated by the door, wondering if she should leave, and he said: 'Please sit down, Charlotte.'

She did so on a settee opposite theirs. He was watching her and she began to feel uncomfortable. Was he doing it deliberately?

'Tell me, Marie,' he said, 'how did your lessons go today?'

She pulled a face. 'All right. I would rather have Charlotte teach me, though,' and she looked impishly across at Charlotte, who smiled.

'I'm not a teacher, Marie,' she said gently. 'Although if you do your lessons as well as you speak English, you have nothing to worry about.'

'I think Marie is rather lazy,' said Jared, but he grinned at his niece as he spoke. 'She needs a firm hand.' Then he looked directly at Charlotte, and there was a challenge in his eyes. It was as if he was daring her to speak up. She had no intention of rising to the bait. So she smiled – and said nothing. Let him do all the talking. How different he was from that gentle stranger she had known so long ago, how very different. She would soon be cured of the hopeless love that had filled her for two years if he carried on as he was doing. And then she might thank him. Perhaps an anonymous gift of ten red roses – the thought was almost appealing. Something must have shown in her eyes, for she saw a muscle tighten in his cheek, an almost imperceptible sign of stress.

'Would you be able to be firm with her?' he asked pleasantly.

'I think so. Marie and I understand one another, don't we?' she asked the child.

'Oh yes. We both love animals – and books.' Marie turned to Jared as she said it.

'Ah, I see! And that is important. Go and tell Mado

78

to bring us something to drink. Milk for you, I think. Charlotte? Coffee – or do you prefer something cool?'

'Coffee would be perfect, thank you,' she answered.

'Coffee for two, and milk for you. Away you go.'

The moment that Marie left the room, Charlotte went to the window and looked out. She couldn't sit still opposite him for a second longer. The vines stretched endlessly away, and nearby an old man in blue vest and denims was busily spraying a plant, pipe firmly planted in his mouth, engrossed in his task.

'Tell me,' he said, 'do you have an evening dress with you?' The question was so completely unexpected that she turned quickly.

'What?'

'I said do you have a long dress with you?'

'Why?' She didn't care if she sounded rude. What business was it of his?

'Because this evening I am having a few friends for dinner.'

'I see. Then Marie and I will be eating in the nursery, I take it.'

'No. You will come down for it.'

'But Madame Grenier told me that when there were guests, Marie and I would eat alone.'

'Not tonight. We will all dine together.' There was a moment's pause, then Charlotte said softly:

'I'm afraid not. I haven't brought anything with me. I don't even possess a long dress.'

She could smile now with relief. The very thought of eating with him and *his* friends could not be borne.

He looked at his watch. 'There's time. We'll go and buy one.' Panic filled her in a blind rush. She moved towards him. He was doing this for some obscure reason of his own, and she was alarmed.

'No,' she said, 'I can't. I don't know anything about prices here, and I have only a little money until my first week is—'

He shrugged and stood up. 'Yes. That's no problem. We'll go after our drink. Marie will come with us and help you choose one.'

She looked at him, then, helplessly, feeling small and powerless in the face of his utter hardness. 'Why?' she asked. 'Why?'

'Because I've invited you, that's why.'

'No,' she shook her head. 'You have some reason — but I don't see—' and Marie came in, followed by the young maid, Mado, carrying a silver tray with coffee pot and cups and saucers.

'Good, then that's decided,' Jared said very pleasantly. 'Drink up, Marie. We're all going out to Macon, and Charlotte is going to buy a dress for herself — and you will help her choose it. How do you like that idea, hey?'

The girl's eyes lit up. 'Oh yes! And do I get a little—' she stopped and bit her lip, still mischievous, waiting.

He laughed. 'A present? Hmm, we'll see. It all depends how well you behave.'

The coffee was scalding hot and went down like fire. He lit a cigarette and sat back and sipped his coffee. Why, oh, why? The question hammered in Charlotte's brain, but he was not going to tell her. She concentrated on her drink, looking at the pattern in the exquisite china saucer, counting the tiny gold roses that covered the brim . . .

'Drink up. We haven't much time,' he said, and she looked up.

'I'll go and wash first.' If she took long enough, the shops would be shut. And he could hardly come and drag her out of her room. She went out, more confident now, ran upstairs and into her bedroom. Safely there, she took off slacks and shirt and washed quickly, immediately feeling cooler and better. Then she found a simple blue dress in the wardrobe and put it on. Then very deliberately, she went and lay down on the bed. It was just a matter of waiting . . .

There was a sharp rap on the door. She waited a second, then called: 'Marie?'

'No. Are you ready?' Jared's voice.

'No, I'm not.' She sat up and hugged her knees. Let him wait.

'How long will you be?'

'Hours and hours,' she said, too softly for him to hear. She heard the handle turn and stood up quickly, nervously. He wouldn't come in, would he? She wouldn't put anything past him.

'Wait a moment,' she said, and crossed to open the door.

'So you are ready.' He looked down at her.

'Yes.'

'Then come on. Time is short. Do you think I'm stupid?'

'Do you want an answer?' She turned her back on him and picked up her bag from a chair, and he stood by the door waiting. She looked up at him then. 'All right,' she said, 'Monsieur de Marais, I'm ready.'

The car was by the front door, and Marie was sitting in the back. It was a long sleek sports car – the one she had seen him get out of in the early hours of that morning. Dark rich blue, it looked capable of great speed, a powerful monster. Just like its owner, she thought as she slid in.

He went at a sedate speed down the drive, along the road, through the village, and then with a quiet roar, opened out. Nothing passed them. Trees and houses blurred dizzily past, and Marie from the back called: 'Lovely, lovely! Faster, Uncle Zhar!'

'This is fast enough for you,' he called. Then to Charlotte: 'Is it fast enough for you?'

'Not as long as you know what you're doing,' she answered, determined not to show any fear.

'Oh, I know what I'm doing all right.' There was something more to the words than their simple meaning, she knew, and her lips tightened. Soon she would hate him. Soon, if he carried on the way he was. Perhaps that was his object.

Then, all too soon, they were on the outskirts of a large town, and he slowed, and turned down quieter streets, then stopped. They were outside a shop with just a few dresses in the window. Charlotte was no expert on clothes, but she needed no one to tell her that these were expensive. She looked at him in faint alarm.

'Not here,' she said. 'I can't possibly—'

'Yes, here.' He was out, coming round to her side, opening the door, and it was no use her sitting there because Marie was already clambering over from the back, pushing her, saying:

'Come on, Charlotte. Oh, isn't this *lovely?*'

Feeling as if she were about to go to her execution, Charlotte stepped out on to the baking hot pavement and looked into the shop. She was terrified. And Jared gave her a cool glance and said quietly: 'In we go, then.'

CHAPTER SIX

'Oh, Charlotte, you look absolutely *beautiful*! Truly. Come and show Uncle Zhar.' Marie tugged her arm, and Charlotte said:

'Wait a moment. I just want to see.' It was odd how quickly her nervousness had left her after they had entered the shop. It might have been something to do with the obvious delight with which Jared was greeted by the proprietress, a tall statuesque woman dressed in black. Or it might have been his own manner, which changed completely once they were inside. Gone the veiled barbs; he behaved in a way that despite herself made her feel less tense. Subtly in charge in an instant, he had spoken quietly to the woman, telling her that Charlotte needed something simple, that everything that could be in any way suitable was to be brought out for inspection.

The woman ushered Charlotte into a large changing room and measured her swiftly and efficiently. There was nothing intimidating in her manner. Clearly Monsieur de Marais was an honoured client, and anyone who came in with him got five-star treatment, Charlotte reflected as dress after dress was brought out for her to see, carried by one of the three young assistants, all it seemed, only too anxious to please.

And then she saw a dress, and pointed to it. 'May I try that one on, *madame*?'

'But naturally. And this as well, *mademoiselle*?' pointing to a deep blue velvet that Charlotte had lingered over, and which had been put to one side. Marie watched wide-eyed as Charlotte tried on first the blue velvet, and then the one she had just seen.

Now she stood in front of the mirror in the changing room and looked at herself, and Marie was urging her to show Jared. It was simple, a long flowing skirt in deepest black, thin belt at the waist and a spectacular blouse top in dazzling white guipure lace. The lace was softly ruffled at the neck, the sleeves were wide, and full, tapering at the wrists to button neatly and demurely. Charlotte didn't need anyone to tell her that she looked good in it, for she *felt* good. But it might be very dear. She had a feeling that it would be expensive.

She allowed herself to be dragged out by Marie, followed by the owner, clasping her hands and exclaiming that never had she seen such a perfect fit.

Jared stood up and looked at them. Then slowly his eyes surveyed Charlotte from top to toe. He nodded.

'Very nice, *madame.*'

'There is a blue velvet—' the woman began, and Charlotte cut in:

'Yes, if you would prefer me to get that—'

'Will you try that on again and show me?'

She turned and went back into the changing room, followed by Marie. She heard their voices as she drew the curtains. Good. They would be discussing prices. If he thought them both all right, he would naturally pick the less costly. She would have to pay back monthly, out of her salary, for she intended sending Aunt Emily as much as she could spare . . . Feverishly changing as she thought, passing the first one to Marie, she slipped on the dark blue velvet again. Sleeveless, thin satin straps supporting the straight bodice that swept out in spectacular fashion into a long full skirt, she liked it as much as the first.

'Oh, Charlotte, you look beautiful in *that* one too,' Marie sighed. 'Is it not difficult to choose?'

'Yes,' Charlotte smiled, 'it is.'

She walked into the shop again and Jared turned slowly and gave her a long keen look. 'Which do you like best?' he said.

Charlotte shook her head, soft hair tumbling round her cheeks. 'I like them both,' she said. 'Either will do. Whichever you—'

He nodded to the woman, who smiled. 'You can get changed now,' he told Charlotte. 'Then we'll go for shoes.'

'Oh no,' she protested. 'I've got some quite decent ones.' The proprietress had vanished towards the back of the shop, and they were alone, for Marie had drifted back to the changing room.

'I insist,' he said calmly. 'Go and change, please.'

Without answering, she went. There was no point in arguing with him, she knew. There was a certain look on his face, and it brooked no disagreement.

She didn't even know which dress he had bought, because it was packed into a huge box in the changing room after she dressed and gone into the shop again to wait with Marie. She wasn't sure if she cared.

He threw the box on the back seat and locked the door again. 'Come on, we'll walk to the shoe shop,' he said. 'It's only round the corner.'

Marie skipped along, holding his hand, and when they passed a sweet shop he told her to wait and went in, leaving both girls outside. He came out with a big heart-shaped box, which he handed to his niece.

'Your present, you little minx,' he said. 'And no eating before meals.'

'Oh, thank you, Uncle Zhar, you are a *darling*!'

'Mmm, you women are all the same. Come on.'

Charlotte was beginning to feel confused. If anyone had once told her she would soon be hurrying through the streets of a French town with a man who was extremely hostile to her, but who had just insisted on buying her a dress for a dinner, that he was now taking her to a shoe shop, she would have said they were mad. But it was happening. In a way it was almost as dreamlike as the village earlier on. Perhaps she *was* dreaming, she thought.

The slippers he chose were real enough. Fragile sandals, a bare couple of strips of silver attached to the sole, they fitted her perfectly, and she nodded.

'Yes, please, I'd like these.'

'And the bag to match,' he told the shop assistant.

'But—' Charlotte protested feebly, and looked at Marie clutching her box of sweets. What was the use? Marie laughed.

'It's no good talking to Uncle Zhar,' she said. 'He doesn't listen.'

A minute later they were on their way back to the car.

She opened the box when she was in her room. She was not alone. Marie had come up with her. Tissue paper hid the dress.

'I wonder which one it is?' said Charlotte, and smiled at Marie. 'Guess.'

Marie looked at her in surprise. 'Don't you *know*?' she said. 'They are both in there.'

'What?' Charlotte gasped, and tore the tissue paper to one side with trembling fingers. 'Oh no!' She sat down on the bed in dismay. 'Oh *no*!'

'What is the matter?' Marie's face held genuine puzzlement.

'I can't afford—' her lip trembled momentarily, and she put her hand to her mouth to hide it.

'Oh, poor Charlotte. It is all right. Uncle Zhar has

treated you.'

'Oh no, he hasn't!' She stood up. 'Where is he, Marie?'

'In his room. But why—'

'Stay there. I'm just going to have a word with him.' She was frightened that if she hesitated, the resolution would be lost.

She knew his room, for Madame Grenier had indicated it on her visit round the château. She knocked on his door and waited, a cold anger growing inside her.

'*Entrez.*' Perhaps he expected one of the servants. She didn't care. He was shaving at a washbasin, naked to the waist, his torso brown and muscular. She faltered, then as he looked across at her, said:

'Why did you get both dresses?'

'Because they both suited you, why else?' His tones was casual, almost amused.

'I can't afford *two*. I don't even know how much one cost – I think you did it on purpose—' He was striding towards her, wiping lather from his face with a towel. He passed her and slammed the door shut.

'You're not paying for them,' he said. 'I am.'

'Oh no, you're not,' she breathed. 'I won't take anything from *you*.'

'Then they cost one franc each, how does that suit you?'

She fought for calm. 'Don't – don't be ridiculous. I know they were very expensive. I'm not a fool.'

'Then consider them as part of a uniform if you like. It's important to keep up appearances, and as I require your presence – to accompany Marie – at certain dinners, it's only fair that you're suitably dressed for the occasion.' He rinsed his face at the bowl and dried it. 'All right? Is that all? I want to get changed.'

'If I'd known, I would have refused to come with you,'

she said.

'Would you? Yes, I think you would. How refreshing to meet someone who's not out for all they can get. Quite a change. Now, I shall have to ask you to leave, I'm afraid, much as I'm enjoying this conversation—' he wasn't even trying to veil the sarcasm, 'as I need to change, and I'm sure you don't want to stay.' And he touched her arm very lightly as though to usher her to the door.

Charlotte stood her ground. 'You're contemptible!' she breathed. 'You're behaving like some lord of the manor who thinks—'

'Why, yes, that's *exactly* what I am,' his eyes glinted hard amber at her, and his face was lean and cruel as he stood there before her. 'Didn't you know? My word is law around here. How do you like that?'

'I loathe you,' she whispered.

'Well, that will do for a start,' he shot back, and took her arm. Without thinking Charlotte instinctively lashed out at him. She caught him a stinging blow on his face.

'Don't ever touch me again,' she said, trembling. 'I told you once before, I don't care *who* you are, you'll keep your hands off me!'

He put his hand to his cheek. 'And if you ever do that again,' he said softly, 'you'll regret it,' and he took his hand away.

'Oh, will I?' she said. Her hand trembled with the urge to strike him, but the anger was deep in his eyes, smouldering dark anger that could erupt at any second.

'Yes, you will.' He stood there very still, waiting for her to move. Unbearable tension filled the room, vibrating round them with almost the quality of sound. As if in a dream, Charlotte turned away, her limbs heavy, like one of those nightmares where you try to run and can't, and something awful, some nameless horror is after you, and a sob escaped her throat and she put her hand up to shield her face as if from a blow, and heard him say:

'Charlotte—' then his hand was on her shoulder pulling her back, and she gasped because she thought he was going to strike her and he was too strong, she couldn't fight him . . .

'Charlotte,' he said it again, and she cried out:

'Oh no, no, stop it!' and pushed at his hand on her shoulder, trying to escape, breathless, helpless, in deperate fear.

'I'm not going to—' he began, but her fear rose in her throat, choking her, and she thought she was going to fall down.

'Let me go,' she said. 'You're too strong for me to fight – I can't—' the room spun round and he caught her and held her.

'I'm not going to hit you,' he said. 'My God, did you think I—'

He was holding her now, and she struggled vainly to escape, like a moth caught in a light's beam, hypnotised, weak. 'Yes, I did,' she managed to get out. 'Why don't you now? You said – no one would dare—' fear gave her the strength to free her hand, to push his chest, and he released her quite suddenly, eyes darker now, mouth a grim line.

'Then go,' he said, 'go now. You're free. What are you waiting for?'

Wide-eyed, she stared at him for several seconds, then turned and ran to the door. A moment later she was in the corridor, and she shut the door behind her and walked back to her own room on very unsteady legs.

Marie jumped up as she went in. 'What's the matter, Charlotte?' she asked.

'Nothing,' she shook her head. 'I have a headache, that's all. I'll be better after a wash.'

'I will go and get something for you. Do not worry. Lie down on the bed.'

'Marie,' Charlotte said weakly, 'I'm supposed to be looking after you, not you after me—'

'Hush! I will be soon back.' Marie swept the box of dresses to the floor and pointed. 'Lie down, please.'

Charlotte obeyed. Her head throbbed painfully. She wished desperately that she could stay there and not go down for dinner, but that was impossible. In a way, Jared was right in what he said. She felt as if she had not the strength to resist him. The thought of trying to defy him by remaining in her room when the gong went was frightening. He would simply come up and make her go down, because for reasons of his own, he wanted her to be at that dinner.

She felt very lost and alone, quite suddenly. She was on her own in a foreign land with no one to turn to for help. No one. Marie was perhaps the most under-standing person, but she was a child, and more, she loved her uncle, that was obvious. And so did I, thought Charlotte softly, but not any more. Not any more. She closed her eyes and waited for Marie to return.

She was ready when she heard the gong. Ready, waiting, and nervous. She had seen two cars arrive, and there could have been more, for it was not possible to see along the front of the château, and some of the engines were as soft and purring as cats. She looked at herself for the last time in the mirror. The blue velvet dress looked better than it had in the shop. Silver sandals peeped out, and she held the bag to her side.

'Charlotte, may I come in?' Marie's excited voice from outside the room.

90

'Of course.' She would feel better going down with her. 'Come in.'

Marie was dressed in a long floral sprigged dress, and looked very pretty. 'Why, you look lovely,' Charlotte told her with a smile.

'*Merci, mademoiselle.*' Marie dropped a curtsey. 'And you look *ravissante!*'

'Thank you.' She looked round, then remembered something. The bottle of perfume that Aunt Emily had bought was on the dressing table. She went and sprayed some on. 'There, I'm ready.'

'Mmm,' Marie sniffed. 'That's *nice.*'

'Good. Let's go.'

Voices came from the dining-room, and Charlotte clutched Marie's hand as they went downstairs. 'Oh, Marie,' she confessed, 'I don't know what to do.'

'Pooh!' said Marie. 'Just stay with *me*. I will look after you – and you look far more beautiful than *anyone,* I can promise you. There will be a lot of silly people who are all very boring. I make games up to myself on these occasions and try to imagine what they would look like in bathing costumes!'

And suddenly, there half-way down the stairs, Charlotte began to see the funny side of the situation. 'Oh, Marie,' she whispered, 'what a lovely idea! You know, I'm beginning to feel *much* better,' and she went on down with the girl at her side, and walked into the crowded room with a smile on her face.

She saw Jared watching her from across the room. Glass in hand, a beautiful blonde at his side, he turned as she came in with Marie, murmured something to the woman by his side, and came towards them. Charlotte took a deep breath. Now was the test. She had to pass it or the evening would be ruined.

'Charlotte, Marie. What will you have to drink?'

'I'll leave it to you, thank you,' answered Charlotte calmly. A fat middle-aged man appeared from nowhere and said to Jared:

'Are you going to introduce me, hey?' Jared bowed and nodded. 'Mademoiselle Lawson, may I present Monsieur Reynaud, an old friend of the family?'

Charlotte took the man's hand and found her own being raised to the other's lips.

'*Enchanté, mademoiselle,*' he leered warmly at her, and Charlotte thought: why, I can soon sort him out! Because the image of him in a bright red swimsuit had suddenly popped into her mind, and it was all she could do not to laugh.

Jared handed her a glass, and Marie one, and she sipped at the sharp aperitif, and listened to Monsieur Reynaud and wondered why she had ever been afraid. And of the scene in Jared's bedroom she thought not at all. She would do so later, but now. She was finding to her surprise that she was actually beginning to enjoy herself.

She thought she knew the reason for Jared's summary invitation later on, as they all sat eating at the long dining-table. The clatter of knives and forks, the chink of heavy crystal glasses and the murmur of voices was all around her and she looked up from the wafer-thin slivers of beef on her plate, together with tiny peas, carrots and potatoes, to see Jared talking to the blonde sitting at his side. She was exquisitely beautiful, a Dresden doll of a woman in a simple black dress that plunged almost to her waist. Her hand rested on his arm for a second, a curiously intimate gesture, and then Charlotte knew. Quite simply, Jared had wanted her to be there to see the woman with whom he was in love.

She felt no pain with the knowledge. There was a strange blankness instead. She was free of him at last.

She turned and spoke to Marie, who sat beside her. 'What time will this evening finish?' she asked.

'I am sent up to bed at eleven – usually,' the girl answered.

'Then I will go with you when you leave,' Charlotte said softly. Let him try and stop her!

Madame Grenier was at the further end of the table, nearly opposite her nephew. Gracious and dignified, she had greeted Charlotte with little surprise, admired her dress and introduced her to some more men and women there. Charlotte wondered what Jared had told his aunt, but it wasn't really important. What was significant, she realized, was the fact that she did not feel overwhelmed by the splendid company she was in. She had imagined she would be nervous, but she wasn't. In a way she was almost indifferent.

After the meal, which lasted until past ten o'clock, the women drifted across to the large salon to drink their coffee, leaving the men in the dining-room. Madame Grenier came over to Charlotte and Marie, as they waited near the door, unsure where to sit.

'Do not forget, Marie, that soon is your bedtime. Do not drink coffee, but have a little wine.'

'Yes, Grand'mère,' the girl obediently replied.

'May I be excused when Marie goes up to bed?' Charlotte said.

'Of course. You have enjoyed your dinner?'

'Very much, *madame*, thank you.'

'Good. My friends are much impressed with our young English lady.' And Madame Grenier allowed herself a little smile.

'Thank you, *madame*.' I wonder, thought Charlotte, if you would smile if you knew about the little game Marie taught me. It had helped, oh, how it had helped!

There were ample chairs for everyone, the staff

brought coffee round, and voices filled the room again, feminine voices. Charlotte looked up from her discussion with Marie to see Jared's woman companion watching her. There was no expression on the other's face, just bright eyes watching her with a strangely cold look about them. You're well matched, Charlotte thought, both cold and hard, and she smiled, and the woman looked away and spoke to the elderly bejewelled matron by her side.

'She is pretty, is she not?' Marie whispered.

Charlotte pretended ignorance. 'Who?'

'Why, Uncle Zhar's friend, Margot.'

'Oh! The blonde lady? Yes, she is very nice-looking.' Charlotte smiled down at her young companion.

'*I* don't like her, and neither does Grand'mère,' Marie whispered.

'Ssh! You mustn't say such things.'

'But it is true. Why should I not say them?'

'Because—' Charlotte struggled to find the most tactful way to explain to this child that it was not wise for her to pass personal opinions of her uncle's friends to someone who was virtually a stranger. 'Because things like that are private, and I'm sure Uncle Zhar wouldn't like you to tell me them. And besides, that lady might be hurt if she knew we were talking about her.'

'Hah! She could not be hurt, that one! She has more money than she knows what to do with, and she is very selfish—'

It was time to stop her. 'Marie, I think it must be nearly bedtime for you – and I'll come up too. We had better go and say good night to your grandmother.'

'Can we talk for a while if we go up now?'

'Just for a few minutes. All right?'

'All right.'

They said their good nights, and Charlotte was

keenly aware that several pairs of eyes were watching them as they left the large room. Her timing could not have been more unfortunate, for Jared was about to enter. He stood to one side to let them pass.

Charlotte looked at him and smiled. 'Good night, Monsieur de Marais. Marie, say good night to your uncle.' He was very dark and attractive in his black dinner jacket and pearl grey tie, and he let his eyes rest on Charlotte as his niece bade him good night and he responded.

'And are you leaving us too, Charlotte?' he asked coolly.

'Yes, I'm very tired. Thank you for letting me come down to dinner, *monsieur*. I found it very enjoyable. It was *very* kind of you to ask me.'

The tone in which she said the words was a study of politeness, but a muscle moved in his jaw, and she thought: Oh yes, he got the message.

'Then good night.'

'Good night.' She took Marie's hand. 'Come, Marie. It's late.'

They walked away to the stairs, and Charlotte didn't look back. She wondered why she had ever thought she loved him.

The next few days were spent almost exclusively with Marie. Charlotte saw little of Jared, and although Yves accompanied them on the horses, it was he who saddled them. They went on a long ride out on Sunday down country lanes, stopping in a small village for long cool drinks. On the return journey, when Charlotte and Marie were riding well ahead, Marie leaned over and whispered: 'I think Yves likes you a lot.'

Charlotte looked quickly at her, to see the mischievous pleasure in the girl's eyes.

'You mustn't say things like that, Marie,' she said.

'Why not?' this in surprised tones. 'It is true. I have seen him look at you.'

So had Charlotte, but she wasn't going to admit it to Marie. 'Well,' she said, 'I think he is very pleasant – and a good driver – but I don't—' she hesitated, 'well, I don't like him in any special way. So I'd rather you didn't talk about things like that.'

'Oh, you *English*,' Marie sighed. 'You are so non-romantic!'

Charlotte laughed. 'You mean unromantic, I think.'

'Yes, that is it. Unromantic. Do you not *want* a boy-friend?'

'Some day, perhaps. I'm too busy looking after you at the moment.' And that effectively ended the conversation. But it stuck in Charlotte's mind – to be dismissed when they returned to the stables, hot and dusty, to be met by Mado, who had clearly been watching for them.

'Mademoiselle Marie,' she called. 'You are to go in to your *grand'mère*, please.'

With a look at Charlotte, Marie slid off her horse's back, helped by Yves, and ran in, followed by the maid.

Yves turned to Charlotte and held out his arms. 'And now you, *mademoiselle*,' he said. It would have been ill-mannered to refuse his offer, and Charlotte allowed him to help her down, unwittingly slightly tense because of Marie's words, which now returned.

He held her too long when she was down, and she tried to pull away. 'Thank you, Yves,' she began, feeling hands on her sides, beginning to move round her back.

'I frighten you?' he said curiously, his dark eyes on her face.

96

'No, of course not, only I – I—' she was silenced as he kissed her very gently, and then he stood back, still holding her, smiling now.

'There – that didn't hurt, did it?'

'Let me go, Yves. You have no right to do that!' She looked round, horrified, and pulled his hands away from her. 'What if someone saw?' Her heartbeat was erratic, her breathing quickened. She had no idea where Jared was, even if he was at home, but the thought of him witnessing what had just happened was one she didn't relish.

Then she heard the voice calling her, Mado's voice 'Mademoiselle Charlotte!' and she was able to escape.

'Coming, Mado.' She fled from Yves without looking back, ran quickly away from him as if pursued, and into the house.

Madame Grenier was in the salon with her grand-daughter. Marie looked round as Charlotte came in, then ran to her: 'Charlotte, I have to go away—'

'*Tiens*, Marie. I will explain to her.' The old woman looked at her.

'Sit down, please, Charlotte. Have a drink of coffee,' then, as Charlotte hesitated: 'Yes, yes, I know you have been riding, and must be hot, but this will not take a moment, and then you may both go and wash.'

Charlotte took the proffered cup and saucer and sat down, waiting for what was to come.

Madame Grenier looked at them both. 'Marie's god-mother, a very dear friend of the family, who lives down south, is ill. We are naturally concerned as you may imagine, and she has expressed the wish to see Marie. I would like you to accompany her for a few days' visit.'

So that was it! So great was Charlotte's relief that the coffee cup trembled momentarily. Visions of dismissal because someone had seen Yves kissing her faded away.

'Oh, *madame*, of course. When will we go?'

'In the morning, I think. You will soon be there. Yves will drive you—' and she stopped as Jared walked in.

'No, Aunt,' he said, 'I think not. I will take them.'

Madame Grenier looked up sharply, clearly surprised at having her wishes countermanded. '*You*, Jared?' She didn't trouble to hide her astonishment.

'Yes, me.' As he looked across the room at Charlotte, she saw what was in his eyes – and she knew, as certainly as if he said the words, that he had seen the incident by the stables. Of course! His room overlooked them! She had not thought to look up. But how did it concern him? She lifted her chin and met his glance.

He looked back to his aunt. 'I was going in a few days anyway. I can go sooner, and kill two birds with one stone.'

His aunt was not pleased, but she hid it well. 'As you wish, of course. Can you be ready in the morning?'

He turned to Charlotte. 'Can *you*?'

'Yes. At what time?'

'Nine.'

'Yes.'

Marie went over to him. 'How nice, Uncle, can we go in the Lamborghini?'

He laughed. 'Of course, and you are to behave yourself.'

'I always do when I'm with Charlotte,' she answered in all innocence, and Charlotte saw the fleeting expression that crossed his face. She could almost have read his thoughts at that moment. Then she realized the full implication of his words.

He was taking them. She stood up and put the empty cup on the table. 'May I go and wash now, *madame*?'

'Yes, yes, off you go – both of you,' They were dismissed with a wave of the old woman's hand. 'Jared, I would like to speak with you a moment.'

And I can imagine what you'll be saying, Charlotte thought, as she and the girl went out. But she had other things on her mind now.

CHAPTER SEVEN

THERE was a storm during the night, so different from those she had known at home in Yorkshire that she went to the window to see it, because sleep was impossible with the thunder reverberating directly overhead. There was little rain, which made the greeny-yellow crackles of lightning even more eerie and frightening. The sky was dense black, lit by those brilliant flashes every minute or so to reveal the outlines of the land in stark silhouette that had a strange beauty of its own. She shivered, holding her arms hugging her sides as she watched. She heard Marie cry out, and quickly went through the adjoining bathroom to the girl's bedroom.

'It's all right, Marie,' she said. 'I'm here.'

'I don't like storms,' Marie answered. 'I can't sleep.'

'We're safe here, love, don't worry.' Charlotte sat on the edge of Marie's bed, and she sat up, long hair tousled, her nightgown gleaming whitely in the shadowy light. 'Just lie down and dream about our journey tomorrow – or rather today.' She caught a glimpse of Marie's clock face as lightning flashed again. 'It's nearly two o'clock. You must try to get to sleep.'

'I would if I had a drink.'

'Oh! A drink of what?'

'Anything. Milk would do. Warm milk.'

Charlotte had never done more than take a quick glance round the huge gleaming kitchen of the castle. She swallowed. Well, now she would have to have a proper look. 'All right, love, I'll get you some. Lie still and count slowly to – to a hundred. All right?'

'Yes.' The little girl lay back sleepily. 'One – two – oh, Charlotte, do I have to count in *English* or French?'

Charlotte laughed. 'English. That will take you longer.' She went quickly back into her own room and put on her dressing gown. Then creeping very quietly so as not to disturb anyone, she went downstairs, along what seemed miles of corridors, and at last reached the kitchen.

Once there, with the light on, she found milk in the refrigerator and switched the electric oven on. Rows of pans hung on the wall and she picked the smallest and began to warm the milk. A search through several cupboards revealed only exquisite china, no beakers. She bit her lip, feeling quite helpless. If the worst came to the worst, she would have to use one. But what if there were an accident? She started on another row of immaculately neat cupboards, bent down to open a door, and a voice said from the doorway:

'What the *hell* are *you* doing here?'

Slowly she turned, and stood up. Jared was angry, that was obvious. He was also wet. His hair gleamed in the light, the shoulders of his jacket were dark with rain.

'I was—' she began, then turned in horror as the rushing sound of boiling milk reached her ears. 'Oh, the milk!' She pulled it away from the heat just in time and switched off. She took a deep breath. 'I was getting a drink for Marie. The storm woke her.'

He looked at her in silence for several seconds. He seemed to be fighting for calm. 'Don't you know that we have servants?' he said at last. '*Nobody* comes down to the kitchens at night. You ring the bell in your bedroom and someone will come.'

She felt suddenly stupid. 'I didn't know,' she managed. 'I mean, I didn't know I'd got a bell. And even if I had I wouldn't have dreamed of ringing it at this time of night.'

'Then I'm telling you that you must. The bells are switched through to Roberts' room at night. He would come to see what you need.'

'There's no point now, is there?' She was getting over the shock of his arrival, and worse, his anger. He couldn't do much worse than he already had, she thought, as she looked back at him. 'I'd like a beaker – if there are any.'

He strode over to a cupboard she had not yet reached, pulled open the door and put a beaker on the working top beside the cooker. 'Is there anything else you need?' he asked, voice heavy with sarcasm.

'Thank you, no, I'll manage.'

'You don't think I'm leaving you here alone, do you? Hurry up and get it done. I'm tired, and I've a long drive in the morning.'

She turned away from him and filled the beaker with the hot milk. Carrying the pan to the sink, she was about to wash it out when he said: 'For God's sake, leave that. Someone will do it in the morning.'

She glared at him. His tone was the last straw. 'Leave me alone,' she said angrily. 'I'll wash it if I want to. I don't take orders from *you*.' And she switched on the tap and filling the pan with hot water, picked up a scouring pad from its dish.

'Oh yes, you damn well do!' and he strode over to her and wrenched the pan from her, sending it rattling into the sink. She threw the pad at him and it landed on his jacket lapel and fell to the floor, leaving a soapy blob. Charlotte began to laugh. She couldn't help herself; she couldn't stop, although she was frightened at his anger.

'You little—' he bit off the expletive and grabbed her firmly with both hands on her shoulders. Shocked, suddenly sobered at his violence, she was jerked into silence. Smouldering eyes met hers and she gasped at what she saw, then the gasp died away as his mouth came down on hers in a kiss of earth-shattering, explosive passion.

Lights burst in her head as she fought for her freedom, loathing him, struggling desperately to get away from the warm lips crushing hers into submission. As easy to escape from an enraged tiger; his hold tightened inexorably and his warm breath was on her face, his arms crushing her; she was powerless to move. She didn't try.

At last he freed her. Shaking, gasping, she fell back against the sink and he said: 'Now why don't you see if Yves can do better?'

She rubbed the back of her hand across her bruised lips. Jared picked up the beaker full of milk and said: 'Come on.'

She thought she had never hated anyone as much as she hated him. She couldn't speak. Trying to keep her steps steady, she went over to the door and went out. She heard him switch the lights off, close the kitchen door, and then he was following her along the wide passage that led to the hall.

She couldn't even run fast enough to get away from him. It took all her strength to merely walk up the stairs. And Jared was close behind her. At her door he handed her the beaker. His face was a blank mask of indifference. 'Goodnight, Charlotte,' he said. 'Sleep well.'

She went in without answering, and bolted the door. Marie lay fast asleep, deaf to the still rolling thunder, her arm flung out, hair fanning the pillow. Softly Charlotte tucked her in, carried the milk to her own room, and drank it. She was crying now, and the tears slid down her cheeks as she swallowed the last drops of warm liquid. Then she climbed into bed, exhausted. A few minutes later she was asleep, the tears still damp on her face.

'You had better take your swimsuit,' Marie suggested, as she watched Charlotte pack some clothes into a small week-end case.

Charlotte looked at her in dismay. 'I didn't bring one,' she said. She didn't add that the only one she possessed was a plain school regulation navy blue.

'What a shame! Never mind, we can buy one in Cannes,' said the fashion-conscious young woman, then added: 'You would look lovely in a bikini.'

'Oh, would I? But what makes you think we'll be going swimming?'

Marie raised her eyebrows. 'Aunt Marie – I am named after her – has a beautiful swimming pool.'

'Of course,' Charlotte murmured. 'Have you packed?'

'Mado has done mine. I am ready.'

'Good. Then shall we go down to breakfast?'

When they had eaten, Madame Grenier appeared and handed Charlotte a bulky envelope. 'Will you be kind enough to give this to Madame Dupont? You are ready for your journey?'

'Yes, thank you, *madame*.'

'And you will phone me when you arrive?'

'Yes, of course.'

'Then everything seems in order. Your cases have

been taken down to the car, and Jared is waiting outside.' She sighed. '*Et alors*, it will be quiet now without Marie.' She led the way through the hall, and the front door was wide open, letting in a golden stream of sunlight. Charlotte blinked as she went out. It was incredible that there had been a storm during the night. Except that the green of the trees was richer and deeper than before, there was no evidence to show that there had been rain. And what of Jared? There was no forgetting what had happened in the kitchen only a few hours before. The memory of her humiliation was burned forever within Charlotte. She hated him now. Even without that final taunt about Yves, she would have loathed him. That had just set the seal on it.

She looked up to see him waiting, standing by the sleek Lamborghini, dressed in fawn slacks and matching open-necked shirt with short sleeves. Sunglasses hid his eyes, but he took them off as they went nearer.

'Good morning,' he said, but only Marie answered. Charlotte couldn't.

Madame Grenier kissed her niece, then shook Charlotte's hand. '*Au revoir, mes enfants*,' she said. '*Bon voyage.*'

Doors slammed, they all waved, and soon the castle was left behind as they sped down the drive.

Marie was in the back and Charlotte sat beside Jared. She still had not spoken to him. She could not avoid it for ever, she knew, and she had no intention of letting Marie see that anything was wrong, but she could not for the life of her have made small talk with the cool dark man by her side. He turned on the radio, and music filled the fast moving vehicle.

'Where are we stopping for lunch?' Marie leaned forward and asked him.

'You'll see when we get there. Is that all you think

about?' he demanded.

'No. But I like you taking me out for meals. It is always so *interesting*.'

'Oh. In what way?'

'The way you make all the waiters rush around. Do you frighten them?'

He laughed. Charlotte would have sworn it was genuine. Perhaps, she thought, he's forgotten about last night.

'No, but I tip them well, that's all.'

'Ah, I see.' Marie nodded wisely. Then, as if remembering, she went on: 'Oh, and we must stop somewhere to buy Charlotte a bikini.'

Charlotte took a deep breath and closed her eyes. No, no, Marie, she said inwardly, but it was too late. 'Why?' Jared asked, and glanced momentarily at her.

'Because she has no swimsuit with her, and Aunt Marie has a beautiful swimming pool.'

'It doesn't matter,' said Charlotte faintly. Perhaps he didn't hear her.

'Then we must stop, of course. Avignon will do, I think, after we have eaten.'

Charlotte clutched her bag. She had sufficient money to buy a costume, and she was absolutely determined that Jared would not go in any shop with her. Marie, yes, but not him. She sat back in the comfortable seat and tried to relax. It would have been a pleasure to travel in a car like this normally. The windows slid open or shut at the touch of a button, the radio was soft and beautifully toned, the seats luxurious. And the air-conditioning ensured that they were not too warm, just pleasantly so.

The road was long and straight, lined with the tall trees so distinctive of French *routes nationales*. They passed heavy lorries loaded with fruit and vegetables, holidaymakers' cars loaded with luggage, and the occasional cyclist plodding steadily along. The sun blazed down on the car and the road ahead so that it shimmered with heat. Charlotte looked back to see Marie lying down with her eyes closed.

'Is she asleep?' Jared asked.

'I think so.' That was the first time she had spoken directly to him, and it was unavoidable.

'Do you want to stop for anything?'

'No, thank you.'

Then there was silence, only the music above the muted roar of the powerful engine filling the car. Charlotte looked out of her side window at the fields and farms flashing past. She still felt the touch of his lips on hers, the crushing, bruising pressure that had left her weak, helpless and angry. I'm glad I don't love you any more, she thought.

'Clothes are dear in this country,' he said. She looked at him.

'It was Marie who suggested I needed a bikini,' she answered. 'Not me. I'm not bothered.'

'But if she goes swimming she'll want you with her.'

Charlotte shrugged. 'Then I'll buy one. Don't worry, Monsieur de Marais, I can afford one.' She saw his jaw tighten and looked away again.

'Do you mind if I smoke?'

'Do you normally ask your servants questions like that?' She couldn't help it. She had vowed to herself to ignore him as much as possible, but the temptation, and the inward bitterness, were too strong to resist.

She saw his hands tighten on the wheel, felt his quick anger, but she no longer cared. He jabbed the cigar lighter button, and reached for a cigarette from the packet in his glove compartment.

A few minutes later he drove off the road and down a quieter side lane, surrounded by fields. Charlotte tensed, wondering why. What was going to happen? But she would not ask.

A village lay ahead of them, and before it was a garage, and at the further side of that a large house at the front of which were tables, shaded by gaily coloured umbrellas advertising popular aperitifs.

He slowed down beside the house, stopped and switched off the engine. Then Charlotte looked at him again.

'We're stopping for a drink,' he said.

'I don't—' she began.

'Don't argue,' he said. 'Just get out. *Please*.' The last word almost grimly.

Silently she obeyed. There had been something in his tone that warned her not to say more.

He walked round to her side. 'What if Marie wakes?' she asked. That was all right, a safe question.

'We'll see her, won't we? Sit down at that table nearest the car. What will you drink? Coke? Aperitif? Lemonade?' He looked down at her and she sensed the enormous power within him, the hidden fire ready to flare up.

'Anything. I'll leave it to you.' She sat down, brushing a leaf from the chair before she did so.

There was silence from the car. He had slowed and stopped very carefully, and perhaps Marie would not wake at all. Charlotte wasn't sure whether she hoped she would or not. She sensed that Jared hadn't finished with her, and he might as well get it over with now instead of smouldering all the way to Cannes.

He came out carrying two glasses of dark brown liquid that fizzed and bubbled. Two straws bobbed in each glass. He sat down opposite Charlotte.

'Coca-cola,' he said. 'Drink up.'

'Thank you.' Ice cubes chinked in her glass, and the drink was refreshing. She didn't realize how thirsty she had been until she began sipping. The silence began to get unbearable, and she stirred uncomfortably. Jared sat there smoking a cigarette and picking up his glass to drink, and he was just looking at her. When she could stand it no longer, she burst out: 'Why don't you say it now?'

He lifted one dark eyebrow. 'Say what?'

'Whatever's eating you. Marie's asleep. Don't think I don't know how angry you are. You make it quite obvious.'

'Do I? That's interesting. And why should I be angry with *you*?'

She took a deep breath. 'You were in the kitchen this morning.'

'And do you expect me to apologize for what I did?'

'You? Apologize? That's something I couldn't begin to imagine,' she answered bitterly. She held the glass tightly. 'I don't know why you insisted on bringing us.'

'I think you do.' His eyes bored into hers now, hard and cool.

She shook her head faintly, overwhelmed. She should never attempt to argue with him. It was impossible to get the better of him verbally, or any other way, for he resorted to brute strength when all else failed, as she had already discovered.

'What, nothing to say?' The voice mocked her.

'No. It's no use, is it? Not with *you*.'

'You're learning fast. Want another drink?'

'No.'

'Then we'd better go.'

She stood up. 'I'll go to the ladies' first. Should I wake Marie?

'No. I'll stop if she wants me to. At the back of the house.' She walked away from him without another word.

When she returned he was in the car, waiting. She closed the door and he drove off, back to the main road. Nothing was resolved, she thought unhappily. It was, if anything, worse than ever.

They stopped for lunch at a place called Le Petit Moulin – The Little Mill – a beautiful restaurant set well away from the road and traffic noises. Water tinkled through the slowly turning mill wheel, and they ate their meal by the fast-moving stream surrounded by trees. The place was obviously well known, and popular, and it was plain that Jared had been there before, for the service they received was first-class in every way.

Marie looked round her with delight, pointing out birds to Charlotte, exclaiming at the huge ginger cat that came to rub its back against the legs of their table. She was wide awake and refreshed after her rest. I wish I was, thought Charlotte. She didn't even feel hungry, although it was nearly two o'clock, and they had been driving for several hours.

Jared sat opposite Charlotte, looking at her as she searched desperately through the menu for something light. 'What will you have to eat?' he asked. His manner, as always when anyone else was with them, was polite and correct.

'I'm not hungry,' she answered. 'Can I just have a coffee?'

'No,' he said. 'You need food, or you'll feel sick. Have an omelette if you can't manage anything else. This place is famous for its omelettes, I assure you.'

'All right. Thank you.' She handed the menu to him. He didn't ask Marie what she wanted to eat. He had merely grinned at her when the menus came, and said:

'You leave it to me, okay?'

'Okay,' she nodded happily.

He ordered, and she sipped at a light clear wine as they waited for the food to arrive. There was a leisurely air about the place, an atmosphere of unhurried calm. White-coated waiters carried dishes to the crowded tables, and a bee buzzed around them searching for flowers, pausing to investigate the roses on their table before wandering away, Charlotte looked at the tall slender vase, holding the three red roses. Red roses. She looked up, and Jared was watching her. She caught her breath. Just for a moment there had been something in his eyes. Something she could not understand. Perhaps he too remembered . . .

He and Marie ate *hors d'oeuvres*, brought on a huge tray from which they chose what they wanted, and Charlotte watched them and drank her wine. What a wonderful place to come with somone you loved, she thought. How romantic the setting, especially at night, for fairy lights were strung across from the trees, and the cool evening breeze would then be scented with flowers. And she was here with him instead.

Her omelette came eventually, light, fluffy and absolutely delicious, tasting delicately of herbs, tiny button mushrooms at the side of the plate. Although still not hungry, she ate it all, and enjoyed it. Marie and Jared had prawns Provençal with vegetables, and the girl tucked in as if starving.

Jared looked at her. 'Well, was it good?'

'Very good, thank you. You were right.'

A trolley loaded with sweets followed, and here Charlotte was sorely tempted by flaky, cream-loaded slices of *gâteau*; luscious strawberries encrusted with sugar; melting, mouth-watering éclairs . . .

Marie had to be restrained from choosing a selection of everything by her uncle, who said sternly: 'We are travelling, remember? One portion only, miss.' To Charlotte he added: 'And what will you have?' very coolly.

It was useless to resist the temptation. The *gâteau* looked too delicious to refuse. She would only spend the rest of the day wondering if it would have been as good as it looked. She told him, and he ordered the same for himself and Marie, who announced that if Charlotte was having it, then so was she. They drank coffee afterwards, and Charlotte found it difficult to keep her eyes open when at last they made their way to the car. In spite of everything, she felt she had to thank Jared. The meal had been superb, no doubt about that, and she told him so.

He accepted her thanks with casual indifference. It made her feel as if she need not have bothered. As they walked to where the car was parked, she looked at him. Tall, broad-shouldered, he strode along with an air of complete self-sufficiency, almost of arrogance. And she saw various women watching him with interested eyes. At her they glanced not at all. It was useless for Charlotte to even try and pretend to herself that she didn't know the reason. She herself had been fascinated by him – once. No more. The cure had been painful, but it had been effective.

It was dark when they arrived at the villa on the hillside high outside Cannes, and it was a blaze of light, like a fairytale palace, long and low and colourful. The car's headlights fanned the hidden shadows of the drive upwards to the front door, and Charlotte sat forward to see it better.

'What a beautiful place,' she said. 'Will Marie's aunt know we're arriving tonight?'

'If I know Aunt Marie, she'll have kept awake especially. The sooner we're in the better.'

Marie, at the back of them, was tired with the travelling, but roused herself to exclaim: 'Oh, this will be a *beautiful* visit! Three of my favourite people, all *together*.' Charlotte didn't know exactly what she meant, but a strange prickle of something ran up her spine, and somehow, Marie's next words came as no surprise. 'Charlotte, Aunt Marie, and you, Uncle Zhar.'

She closed her eyes. Oh no, don't let him say anything – cruel, she thought.

'That's good. So your behaviour should be something special, eh, little one?'

'Oh yes, of course. I am always good, aren't I, Charlotte?'

Charlotte laughed. 'Of course you are.'

The door was flung open and a white-jacketed manservant came down the steps to greet them.

'Madame Dupont is waiting your arrival, *m'sieur*,' he told Jared, who opened the door for Charlotte and Marie.

'We'll go right up to see her, Henri. Right away.' Jared turned to Charlotte. 'You will come too, she's looking forward to meeting you.'

'And I have an envelope for her from Madame Grenier,' and she held it up.

They went into a wide hall whose floor was a vast expanse of polished black and white tiles. White louvred doors led off from both sides, and the hall was dominated by a white statue of the Winged Victory in the centre. A white marble staircase with delicate gold and black wrought iron balustrades led upwards to the left, and Henri led them up to a room at the front, knocked and waited.

'*Entrez*.' The voice came instantly in response.

Charlotte waited just inside the door while Jared and Marie went across the pearl grey carpet to the huge bed. Aunt Marie was not remotely what she had expected. Visions of someone similar to Madame Grenier vanished for ever as she gazed at the huge resplendent woman lying propped up on a sea of pillows in the bed. Immaculate blonde hair was elaborately curled – not one out of place, it seemed, and Aunt Marie's face was split in a huge welcoming smile as she greeted first her goddaughter, then Jared.

'Oh, my dear – and Jared too! Why this honour?'

'How could I miss my favourite woman?' he rejoined lightly. 'I think you've brought us here under false pretences, you old fraud.'

Her laughter boomed out. 'Ah, but I'm better for seeing you. These stupid doctors – they know nothing at all, I tell you. They say I must rest, and not eat so much, or—' and then she saw Charlotte. 'So! You let your English miss wait by the door while you talk. Shame on you! Come and say hello, my dear.'

Charlotte went forward to shake the woman's hand, to smile into a pair of startlingly bright blue eyes that were as guileless as a child's, and as full of fun.

'So you are Charlotte, hey? And they did not tell me you were beautiful. *Now* I know why Jared came with you!' And the hearty laugh came out again, joyously full of life. Charlotte felt herself go warm. Jared, without a pause, said:

'I had to come down anyway, I have to see old Mercier on business – tiresome but necessary – and you never invite me here, so I have to invite myself.'

Seen close to, it was clear that Aunt Marie was in her sixties. Wrinkles were concealed by make-up, and the immaculate hair was an elaborate wig, and yet strangely enough there was a beauty about her, and Charlotte sensed instinctively that she was a person that everyone loved and trusted.

'Madame Grenier gave me an envelope for you, *madame*,' she said, handing the bulky package over into a heavily beringed hand.

'Ah! You will call me Aunt Marie, no? That is better. We are all one family while we are here, eh, Jared?'

'As you say, Aunt,' Jared agreed, and he was smiling. 'But now your family is going to leave you to get some sleep, or your doctor will shoo us away tomorrow, and—'

'All right, don't go on. You always were bossy, even as a child!' The old woman winked at Charlotte. 'Don't let him bully you, my dear!'

Oh, if only you knew, thought Charlotte, but she smiled, and shook her head. 'No, I won't, *ma* – Aunt Marie.'

'Good! Then off you go. There is food ready for you. Henri will look after you. And in the morning I expect to see my little Marie again, and we will breakfast together.'

'Yes, Aunt,' Marie leaned over to kiss her godmother. 'Goodnight, sleep well.'

'And you too, child. Away you go now. I feel better already.'

Supper had been set out for them on a small round table in a room whose picture windows looked out now into pitch-black night, but, Marie assured Charlotte, overlooked the swimming pool.

Henri hovered round them, concerned that everything should be just right, telling Jared that their cases had been taken up to their rooms, that Madame Dupont would undoubtedly start to improve now . . .

Charlotte's head swam with tiredness, but she drank coffee and ate wafer-thin sandwiches in an effort to keep awake long enough to reach her room.

Jared looked at her and frowned. 'Are you all right?' he asked.

'Yes, thanks. I'm just tired, that's all.'

'So is Marie. Hey, child, don't go to sleep here.' But Marie's eyes were closing and she smiled dreamily and snuggled down into her chair. Jared stood up. 'Time to go.' He picked his niece up and carried her out of the room, followed by Charlotte, who thanked Henri and wished him good night as he held the door open for them to go through.

She and Marie had adjoining rooms, each with its own bathroom. Jared put Marie down on her own bed and turned to Charlotte. 'Can you manage?' he asked.

'Yes, thanks.' She waited for him to go.

'All right. I'll see you in the morning.'

'Yes. Good night.' He didn't move, merely stood looking down at the inert figure on the bed as if debating something.

Charlotte felt uneasy. Without considering why, she went to the door and opened it. 'I *can* manage,' she repeated. 'And I'm very tired. Thank you for bringing Marie up.'

He turned towards her and for a moment she saw a look in his eyes that set her heart pounding in her breast. She couldn't look away, his glance held her, and tension vibrated round them. Then he walked towards her, and for a moment she feared that he would touch her. Instinctively she backed away from him, nervous, and he spoke, his voice harsh.

'I'm not going to touch you,' he said. 'Did you think I was?'

'I wouldn't know,' she answered. 'I don't know *anything* about you, do I? Why don't you go?'

Without another word he walked out. She closed the door after him, and leaned against it. She was weak and trembling, but she didn't understand why. She hoped that she would see very little of him during the next few days. Hate him she might, but he had the power to disturb her deeply. She went over and began to undress the sleeping child.

CHAPTER EIGHT

Rich, muddled dreams filled Charlotte's sleeping hours. A road vanishing under the wheels of a super fast car, an old woman by a swimming pool whose laughter boomed out as she told Charlotte that Jared was madly in love with her, that that was why he had brought her . . .

She woke up suddenly because a maid was standing by her bedside smiling down shyly at her.

'*Bonjour, mademoiselle.* Your breakfast is here.' She struggled to sit up, only too aware that she wore a thin cotton nightie she had made herself, and that it was woefully unsuitable for the opulent bedroom that was hers.

'Thank you. What time is it?'

'It is nearly nine, *mademoiselle.* Marie is already with Madame Dupont. You are to take your time, she says. Shall I run your bath?'

'Yes, please.' Charlotte smiled at the girl. 'What is your name?'

'I am Lucia, *mademoiselle.*' The girl was Italian, she realized that now. There was the trace of accent in her French, and she had dark Latin eyes.

'Thank you, Lucia.' Charlotte took the tray from the girl, and began buttering a flaky *croissant.* The coffee in the pot was scalding hot and black, and she added to it from the tiny jug of milk and sipped gratefully.

Lucia vanished silently. I shall have to write to Aunt Emily, thought Charlotte. She'll never believe this place. I'm not sure if I do myself. She was looking forward to seeing it from the outside in daylight, and the swimming pool she had heard so much about. The thought of that brought back the memory of their stop in Avignon the previous afternoon. Jared had pulled up in a quiet street and turned to Charlotte.

'Off you go,' he said. 'The shop's down there. Are you going, Marie?'

'Yes. May I, Charlotte?'

'Of course.' So he had no intention of coming with her anyway. 'I'll be as quick as possible.'

'Take your time,' he had replied indifferently. 'I'll buy an evening paper and read it,' and he had got out and strode back to a newspaper seller on a corner.

It hadn't been a bikini after all, because they were ridiculously expensive, but there had been a sleek-fitting black swimsuit that Charlotte knew immediately was the one she wanted. She could afford it too, and had tried it on, knowing it would fit. It did, perfectly.

They went back to the car, and Jared opened the door, putting the newspaper he had been reading to one side. 'Get one?' he asked with no trace of interest in his voice. 'Good. We'll go.' And that had been that.

Today, if Marie wanted a swim, she would wear it for the first time. The important thing, of course, was that she would be spending a lot of time with her godmother, the reason for their visit in the first place.

So it was a pleasant surprise, when at last Charlotte went down, a little unsure of where she should go, to be met by Henri. Perhaps he had been waiting for her. 'Mademoiselle Lawson,' he said, 'Madame Dupont and Marie are by the pool. Follow me, please.'

He led her out of the front door, along a gravel path and round to the back of the villa. Green shutters were flung back, all windows open to let in the sun. The grass was a rich green that almost hurt the eyes, and perhaps the lushness was partly due to the sprinklers that set off a constant rainbow sparkle of water at intervals across its vastness. Bushes and shrubs full of flowers provided relief from the greenness of the lawns, reds and pinks, mauves and yellows, a profusion that was too much to take in all at once. Charlotte sighed, and the man heard, and turned his head slightly, and he smiled.

'Mademoiselle slept well?'

'Oh yes, thank you. I was just looking at all this,' she waved an arm. 'It's almost too much to take in.'

'Madame Dupont likes beautiful things around her,' he said, and there was a slight smile on his face as he said it – and she didn't understand it. 'Wait until you see the pool. I think you will find that agreeable.'

'Hello! Charlotte, I am here!' Marie's voice greeted her as they rounded the back of the house, and Charlotte stopped in wonder – and just looked.

The pool was kidney-shaped, filled with sparkling blue water, and Marie was splashing about, her long hair streaming out, a glimpse of a multi-coloured floral costume as she jumped up and down in excitement. Coloured paving stones surrounded the pool, and several comfortable chairs were dotted about, topped by sunshades. In one was Madame Dupont, who waved.

'Come and sit down, Charlotte,' she called. 'Henri, drinks, please.'

'Yes, *madame*.' He melted away, and Charlotte skirted the water to sit beside the old woman. A light rug covered her legs, and a huge red umbrella shaded her from the sun's glare.

It was a relief not to see Jared. Charlotte sat down in an adjoining seat, and sank back into the cushions.

'Well, and how did you sleep, hey?'

'Very well, thank you,' Charlotte smiled.

'That is good. Jared offers his apologies, but has had

to go into Cannes on business. I told him that it is ridiculous to think of work in this weather, but—' she shrugged. 'Men! They cannot be told anything.'

'No,' Charlotte murmured in polite agreement. She didn't want to talk about Jared. She was to be disappointed.

'Still, he will return soon, I dare say.' A look from those startlingly blue eyes, and Charlotte was unable to look away. 'He is no fool, that Jared.' She bit her lip. The old woman's meaning was obvious – especially remembering her remarks the previous night. Marie was out of earshot, making her way up the pool in a puppyish breast stroke, clearly proud to be showing off her swimming prowess. Charlotte felt the need to put Aunt Marie right on one or two points – but how to begin?

'Er – *madame*—' she began, only to be interrupted by the other's:

'Aunt Marie, if you please!'

'Aunt Marie, Jared is not— er – he doesn't—' Oh, where were the words? 'I mean, he has a girl-friend—'

Laughter boomed out, hearty and unrestrained. 'Ah! He has, has he? Tell me, is it the delectable Margot?'

She knew her! 'Yes,' said Charlotte, relieved. Surely there would be no need now for further explanations?

'So? And you have met her? So tell me, what do you think of her, hey?'

Charlotte shook her head, dismayed. This was getting worse with every moment that passed. 'She seems very – nice,' she said at last.

Those blue eyes were too shrewd to be fooled. 'She is nice? Hmm, her parents have a villa near here, and I have met her more than once. Nice is not a word I would use, but perhaps you are a kind person – yes, I think you must be – Tell me, did Jared tell you anything about me?'

The sudden change of subject startled Charlotte. 'No,' she said. 'I only know you are Marie's godmother, and one of her favourite people.'

'I am? Good! Marie and I have always had good *rapport*. We are of an age, she and I – I still see things with the eyes of a child. Does that surprise you?'

'No.' Charlotte looked at her and smiled. 'I felt when I first met you last night that you—' she hesitated, wondering if it was good manners to express personal opinions.

'Yes? Go *on*.' Just like Marie, impatiently.

'Well, that everyone who met you must like you.'

'Why, thank you, child. I see you are a young woman of shrewd judgment.' But even though she said it half jokingly, Charlotte knew the older woman was pleased.

Drinks came, brought out by another maid carrying a silver tray, with matching silver jug and three tall glasses. A bowl of ice cubes with tongs was set out on a low table as well, and the maid bobbed a curtsey and departed quietly. Aunt Marie gestured. 'I'll let you pour out, Charlotte,' she said. 'So Jared didn't tell you about me, hmm? So you expected a dear old lady, I suppose?'

'Well—' Charlotte bit her lip. 'Yes, I suppose I did.'

'And you saw me?' Her laughter echoed round the pool, and Marie turned round in surprise, then waved.

'Come on out, little one,' Aunt Marie called. 'We have a drink for you.' She went on, as Marie scrambled out of the pool: 'I shall never be an old lady, *dieu merci*. I do not allow age to interfere with my enjoyment of life. I am a widow now, with four daughters, seven grandchildren – they live far away, but often come to visit me

– you remind me very much of my second granddaughter, Angeline, a sweet girl – where was I? Oh yes, I have had a full and interesting life, and I wouldn't change a minute of it, and not many people can say *that*.' And then, as Marie ran up, shaking herself and scattering drops all around her, she continued, without a change of tone: 'I was a dancer in the Folies Bergère when I met and married my dear husband.' Charlotte tried to hide her astonishment, but Aunt Marie chuckled. 'Yes, I can see your surprise. *Et alors*, I was a very respectable girl, I assure you. My *maman* chaperoned me constantly, and my life was possibly quieter than most. Then Jacques came on the scene, and whisked me away on a honeymoon that lasted a year, then we came and lived here, and here I have been ever since.' She stopped and waited as Charlotte handed her, and then Marie, a glass full of sparkling lime cordial.

'Ah, lovely. Now Marie, drink up, and then dry yourself or you will take a cold. There are plenty of towels in the changing rooms.'

'Yes, Aunt.' The girl sipped her drink obediently, put it down on the table with the words: 'I'll finish it when I come back,' and ran off to the other side of the pool where there was a row of doors set in the long white building. She vanished through one, and for a few moments there was silence.

'So you see,' went on the old woman, 'that is my life. And I constantly get lectures from my doctors on taking it easy, and eating less – and all sorts of boring things. Already I am better for seeing you all – they know nothing, these stupid men, but I let them have their say. It is one way for them to earn a living, I suppose! And besides, every so often, if I feel a little lonely, I can send for my dear ones – nobody dares refuse poor old Aunt Marie when she is poorly!' The chuckle grew to a laugh, and Charlotte found herself irresistibly joining in.

'Oh,' she managed at last, 'I think Jared was right. You are a fraud!'

'Yes, I am.' Then the old woman's voice changed, became quieter. 'And now tell me. What is wrong with you and Jared, hey?'

'Wrong?' Charlotte swallowed. Her hostess had a most disconcerting habit of switching subjects in a matter of seconds. 'I don't see—'

'Rubbish! I have never seen him so jumpy before. I wondered, and then I saw you standing by the door, and I thought, aha!'

'Oh no, *madame* – I mean Aunt Marie,' Charlotte said hastily. 'You are mistaken, I'm sure. Jared doesn't like me at all, and I certainly don't like him – oh, I'm sorry, I shouldn't say that – he's a r-relative of yours—'

'Say what you like! This is just you and me talking, and will not go any further, that I can promise you. And may a nosey woman who should know better ask you *why* you don't like one another, hey? Here you are, a beautiful young woman with a good sense of humour – important, that – and he a *most* attractive specimen of manhood – let's be in no doubt about that, he *is* – and there you are both sending off very disturbing vibrations across the room – oh yes! I felt them, so no use to pretend.'

And Charlotte looked at her, and saw not just plain curiosity but a kindly concerned look in those blue eyes. And she knew that here was someone she could tell the truth to. All the pain, the hurt she had had to keep within her for so many days because she was alone in a strange land came bubbling to the surface, and she said:

124

'When I went to work for Madame Grenier at the château I had no idea that Jared would be there. You see, I had met him two years previously when I was on holiday in Paris with my aunt . . .' And thus she began the story that had begun at that fateful party, and never really finished.

The older woman listened in fascinated silence until they were interrupted by Marie, when she asked her to go into the villa to find her shawl, and told Charlotte to go on.

At last the tale was done, for there was not really much to it after all, and Charlotte felt surprisingly light with relief when she had finished. Aunt Marie turned to her and spoke softly: 'Oh, my dear girl, my dear Charlotte, thank you for telling me.' She shook her head. 'That man!'

'Please – *please* don't say anything,' begged Charlotte.

'Ah! No. That is definite – tell me again, when *exactly* was it that you met him in Paris?'

'The end of June – exactly two years ago, almost to the week,' Charlotte said, and realized with a pang that it was precisely to the day – tomorrow would be the second anniversary of their meeting. How strange!

'Yes, I thought so.' Aunt Marie nodded sagely, as if something had been confirmed. 'I remember the time well.'

Charlotte looked at her, puzzled by what was in her tone, but Aunt Marie smiled. 'It is my birthday on Friday,' she said. 'So of course it is a time of year I always remember.' But Charlotte was left with the feeling of something else left unsaid. Something important.

'Thank you for taking me into your confidence,' the old woman said after a moment. 'I appreciate it, and I will respect it, have no fear.'

Then Marie ran out from the house, followed by a tall thin worried-looking man carrying a black bag.

'Madame Dupont,' he began, 'I am *most* distressed to see you out here.'

'My doctor, or one of them,' the older woman whispered loudly to Charlotte, 'a real old fusspot, I'm afraid.' Then, in a much lower voice: 'Ah, Doctor, I feel much better today, you see, now that some very *dear* people have come to visit me . . .'

Charlotte stood up, smiled at the doctor, and said, 'If you will excuse me—' and walked back into the villa with Marie.

Aunt Marie's ringing tones followed her – 'Come back soon, I will get rid of this bossy man in a few minutes—' They fled.

Dinner that evening began quietly. Jared had returned in the middle of the afternoon and gone swimming with his niece. Madame Dupont had come out again well after lunch assisted by Charlotte, and sat herself down by the pool to watch them. Charlotte had used the excuse of a headache to avoid going into the pool with him, although she longed to plunge into the cool blue water. Instead, she sat beside the old woman, who reminisced about old times, old friends, and journeys over the world. It was difficult for Charlotte to avoid watching Jared and he dived and swam like a fish, and took Marie for rides in the water. He was built like an athlete, splendidly muscular, perfectly proportioned, looking like some dark Adonis as he paused at the side of the pool before scything through the water yet again.

Now, sitting with him at dinner, Charlotte looked across at him and wondered what he would think if he knew that she had told Aunt Marie all about their brief romance in Paris. He would, she felt sure, be furious. She no longer cared.

They were waited on by Henri and the dark Italian girl Lucia, and the food was superb, as it had been at lunch.

Conversation was general, and pleasant, and then, towards the end of the meal, Aunt Marie dropped a bombshell. Very casually she said:

'Ah, I have just remembered! I have two tickets for a grand ball in Cannes tomorrow. Very expensive, I might add, and *very* difficult to get hold of – and now that I am not allowed out I cannot go. So, Jared, why don't you take Charlotte?'

Charlotte froze, looked wide-eyed at the old woman, and felt a wave of sheer horror sweep over her. What on earth did she think she was doing?

Jared looked at her too, but there was nothing on his face to give him away. '*You* were going? With whom?'

'Does it matter now?' the old woman retorted. 'And do you think I am too senile to enjoy myself? You sound astonished.'

Good for you, thought Charlotte, hiding a smile. Jared might be able to boss everyone else about, but in Aunt Marie he had met his match.

'No. I beg your pardon, Aunt. Of course I didn't think that for a moment. But I didn't think you enjoyed the kind of occasions where, to use one of your own expressions, "everyone is decorated like a Christmas tree".'

'Did I ever say that? Hmm, maybe I did. Anyway, you've not answered my question yet. Why don't you and Charlotte go?'

'She may not want to,' he replied very evenly. 'Do you want to go to a "grand ball" tomorrow, Charlotte?'

127

'I've never been to one before,' she answered. Now the onus was on her. A refusal would seem ungracious – even though Aunt Marie must surely *know* how she felt, after their talk that morning. 'And I've nothing to wear.'

'You should have brought your dresses with you,' chimed in Marie helpfully.

Charlotte looked to the old woman in appeal. 'It's true, Aunt Marie,' she said. 'I have nothing to wear.'

'My dear, there is a wardrobe full of superb gowns upstairs!' was the surprising reply. 'You and I will go after dinner and look at them.' Was there to be no escape? The subject was dropped then, but when they eventually went upstairs to a large bedroom covered in dust-sheets, Charlotte turned to Madame Dupont.

'Oh, please,' she said, 'tell me why you've asked Jared to take me out tomorrow?'

'Because I would have done so if you *hadn't* told me what you did.' The old woman seated herself heavily on the bed. 'And it is true, the tickets are very expensive, and would only have been wasted – and I *hate* waste, and thirdly, my dear child, quite simply, it could be a good evening out for you. Jared will be a good escort, I can promise you that. He has manners, that one – and he will not risk my displeasure by behaving badly.'

Charlotte felt mean. She went over to the old woman and sat beside her. 'I'm sorry,' she said. 'I just thought that perhaps you were trying to–' she stopped.

'Who? *Me?* Trying to push you together, you mean? *Mon dieu*, no, I would not be so cruel, when it is so obvious that you and he are poles apart in every way!' Aunt Marie chuckled. 'It is selfish of me really. As *I* cannot go, I want you to go instead and tell me all about it. That is all.'

Charlotte stood up. 'I'll look at the dresses if I may,'

she said, and went to the long wardrobe covering one wall. She didn't see the expression on the other's face.

'There is a collection from years, I must warn you,' her voice came as Charlotte slid open the doors. 'And some belonging to my daughters and granddaughters too. So you see, there must be *something*.'

Charlotte gasped at the glittering display before her eyes. A long row of every kind of dress hung there, all colours, different lengths, some sparkling with silver or gold threads, others in plain muted shades. Rows and rows of shoes lay neatly at the bottom of the wardrobe.

Charlotte began to laugh. 'I don't believe it!' she gasped. 'There are even more here than in the shop Jared took me to.'

'Take a look, pull them out, and then try on those you like. It will be interesting to see if your taste is similar to Angeline's, will it not?'

There was a tap on the door, and Marie peeped round. 'May I come and look?' she asked.

The next hour passed quickly – and quite delightfully. It was so different from the shop in Macon, when Jared had been waiting and watching. Here she was relaxed, and in a way, at home, with just Marie and her godmother commenting and admiring. Madame Dupont told the story of each dress as Charlotte took it out. That one had been worn by her daughter at a very grand ball in Paris several years ago at which President de Gaulle had been guest of honour. This one worn by Angeline at a yacht party in Monte Carlo with foreign Royalty present, and this one – ah! Aunt Marie sighed as Charlotte lifted out an exquisite red velvet gown in Regency style, rich and yet simple in design, with short puffed sleeves.

'That one,' she said, 'bring it to me, my dear. That

was mine – years ago,' she began to laugh at Marie's startled gasp. 'Ah yes, my child, I was as slender as Charlotte in those days. You do not believe, hm? Well, I can hardly blame you, but ah, what memories that dress brings back! Do me the honour of trying it on, please, Charlotte.'

'Of course,' Charlotte smiled. She had to stoop slightly for Marie to fasten three tiny buttons at the back, then she stood up and walked slowly towards Madame Dupont, seeing the memories in the old woman's eyes, the wistful nostalgia of days long past and gone . . .

'It's simply beautiful, even today. I am astounded!'

'Charlotte, you look much nicer than you do in those others,' Marie exclaimed.

It was a perfect fit in every way. It might, Charlotte thought, have been made for her. A faint lavender scent clung to it, and she looked across the room and took a look in the long mirror, and caught her breath. For a second she hadn't recognized herself. She saw only a tall slender girl standing there – and then she went closer to the glass, and it was really her. She laughed.

'I wasn't sure if it was me,' she said.

'Do you like it?' Madame Dupont asked.

Charlotte turned to her. 'It's the most beautiful dress I've ever tried on in my life,' she said simply.

'Then it is yours to keep. And you will wear it tomorrow?'

'Of course, with great pleasure – but I can't possibly let you give—'

'Nonsense! Do you think I shall ever wear it again? Nothing would make me happier. *Alors*, that is decided. Now, try on some of those ridiculous sandals, and let us see which go best.'

CHAPTER NINE

THE pool was pleasantly cool, and both Marie and Charlotte swam and splashed happily the following morning, watched by Madame Dupont from her usual place on the terrace. As they swam to the side for drinks, she told Charlotte: 'I have phoned my hairdresser to come and do your hair before this evening.'

Charlotte was too astonished to speak for a moment, then managed: 'Thank you, but I was going to wash m-my hair this afternoon—'

'Yes, and I'm quite sure it would look fine, but allow an old woman to have her own way in some things.'

Charlotte laughed as she scrambled out. 'I thought you said you would never be old,' she said.

'I am whenever I want my own way,' Madame Dupont said complacently. 'So that is settled. Madame Claire will arrive at six, and then at nine you will depart for the Grand Ball.'

Charlotte took a long sip of her drink and thought about that. She had managed to put all disquieting thoughts about the evening ahead out of her mind, but Madame Dupont now brought it all back. For her sake she would try and enjoy it, and store up as many memories as she could to tell her the following morning, but Charlotte had to admit that she was not looking forward to having to spend so many hours in Jared's company. How could she, after all that had happened? The scene in the kitchen at the *château* still rankled. She would never, she thought, forgive him for what he had done, the bitter contempt with which he had kissed her. For that was what it had been, she realized now; he despised her.

She looked up, and the old woman was watching her with a very knowing look in her eyes, almost as if she knew her thoughts.

'Don't worry,' she said.

Charlotte smiled, shaking her head. 'No, I won't,' she answered softly. But it was easier to say than to do. And as the hours passed, she grew more apprehensive.

It was nearly nine – the fateful hour. Charlotte, who had not eaten a bite since lunch at two, felt faintly sick. She wished desperately that she did not have to go, but it was too late for that; her hair was done, the dress was on, and Madame Dupont had spent nearly an hour giving her the most astounding make-up tips, and watching them put into practice. She was seated at the dressing table in her room, Marie at one side, Aunt Marie at the other, and the old woman was sitting forward on her chair as Charlotte put the finishing touches to her eye shadow.

'No, *smooth* it in, child, there, just above the eyelid. Ah! That's it,' she sat back as if a hard task had just been completed, and looked appraisingly at Charlotte. 'Hmm, that *is* it. You look superb. You did not think I knew so many tricks, did you?'

Charlotte looked at herself. A cool blonde beauty gazed back at her from the mirror, someone whose eyes were dark and sparkling, whose mouth was as richly red as the fabulous dress that she wore.

'I don't believe it's me,' she said faintly. 'It is, isn't it?'

'It is.' Madame Dupont stood. 'Come, we will go and show Jared.'

He was waiting in the hall. As Charlotte slowly walked down, he looked up. She saw the sudden shock in his dark eyes, the tension he could not hide immediately, and she was satisfied. It had shown on his face, just for the instant before he managed to conceal it; he was sharply aware of her as a woman. There was a sense of power in the knowledge.

Madame Dupont's voice from the top of the stairs shattered the fragile mood.

'Come and help an old lady down the stairs to see you off,' she called.

Jared waited until Charlotte reached the last step, then ran up to where his aunt waited with Marie. They came slowly down, and as Charlotte looked up, Aunt Marie closed one eye in a huge wink. The other two didn't see it, only Charlotte, who smiled in acknowledgment.

They all went to the door where Aunt Marie kissed first Charlotte, then Jared. 'Have a lovely evening, *mes enfants*,' she said. 'And remember, I want a full report in the morning.'

'Yes, I promise,' Charlotte answered.

'And you have the tickets safely, Jared?' she asked.

'Yes.' He patted the pocket of the white evening jacket he wore. He was immaculate, his tan accentuated further by the dazzling whiteness of lacy shirt front, black bow tie at his neck, dark hair brushed back, powerful features with an inscrutable expression. Now – but not before – not for an instant of time when she had seen what she had seen. And Charlotte smiled to herself.

He spoke when they were half way down the drive.

'That dress suits you,' he said.

'Does it? Thank you. Madame Dupont has given it to

me. That's three evening dresses I have now,' she answered.

He negotiated the bends in the drive with care, and once away from the house, darkness rushed in and surrounded them, leaving only the powerful twin beams from the headlights to show them the way. Through the gateway, down the path to the main road into Cannes they went, and he spoke not another word.

It was a beautifully clear night, with a sickle moon high over the Mediterranean. A night for lovers, thought Charlotte, and here we are together, only we hate one another, we're only going to please an old woman. And she sighed, only a tiny sigh, but he heard it, and said sharply: 'What's the matter?'

She had already decided that come what may, she would not get involved in any argument with Jared, so she answered, with bright determination:

'Why, nothing, I was just thinking what a lovely night it was.'

'And are you looking forward to the evening?'

She might not be going to argue, but she saw no reason to lie. 'No,' she answered. 'But then I don't think you are, are you?'

She saw his shrug in the dark. 'I came to please Aunt Marie – as you did. She is a woman who usually manages to get her own way in things – as you may have noticed.'

He waited at the edge of the main road for an opportunity to ease into the stream of traffic, and the minute he had done so, Charlotte answered him. 'Perhaps she does. But then I imagine everyone would want to please her. She's one of the nicest people I've ever met.'

'I wasn't attempting to criticize her, merely stating a fact,' he said coolly. 'I'm very fond of her myself.'

'It's her birthday on Friday,' Charlotte said, because

there had been a slight something in his voice that threatened to start the argument she was so determined to avoid.

'My God, so it is! When did she tell you?'

'When we were talking about—' and she suddenly remembered exactly what they had been discussing, and went hot and cold as she fumbled for words. 'About th-things yesterday.' She hoped he didn't notice her stammer of confusion.

If he did, he didn't comment on it, merely said: 'I must get her a present.'

'Are there any shops near the villa?' she asked.

'No. The nearest are in Cannes itself. Why, do you want to get her something?'

'Perhaps Marie and I can go down and get her a little gift,' she answered. 'Tomorrow.'

'Walk it, you mean? You must be joking.'

'I wasn't. I don't know how far it is, do I?' she answered reasonably enough.

'I'll take you both tomorrow afternoon,' he said. 'I can spare an hour.'

She felt her mouth tighten at his tone. Swallowing hard, she said: 'Thank you.'

'Don't mention it.' He jabbed the cigar lighter button in and lit a black cheroot. 'We're nearly there,' he told her. 'Aren't you nervous?'

Did he expect her to be? Of course he did. He would be delighted if she were. Charlotte took a deep breath. 'They're only people, aren't they?' she asked in a mild tone. 'Are they so very grand and important that I should be shaking in my shoes?'

'You said yourself that you'd never been anywhere like this before,' he answered, avoiding a direct answer. 'It must be strange.'

'Of course it will be. But no more so than going down

to meet guests at dinner in your home – as you insisted I did, if you remember. For that I must now thank you, I'm sure *that* experience will be a help to me tonight.' And she smiled in the darkness of the car. She felt almost lightheaded, partly due to hunger, no doubt, but also in a strange way because she was rapidly regaining confidence.

He laughed, not entirely without amusement. 'I'll say one thing for you,' he remarked. 'You're very good at giving your answers.'

'I've learnt a lot since I came to France,' she answered. 'One way or another.' The last four words were said in a very dry tone, and let him take that how he chose, she thought.

'I'm sure you have. Do you like working for my aunt?'

'Madame Grenier? Yes. I like Marie very much as well.'

'It may be only a temporary post. Marie may be sent to a boarding school when she's a little older – we haven't yet decided.'

'Oh *no!*' the words were wrenched out of her in a shock of dismay.

He said sharply: 'What do you mean?'

She stiffened in her seat. Perhaps he thought – 'I know the post is a temporary one,' she said quickly. 'I knew that when I took it. That wasn't why I was shocked.'

'Then what? Because of boarding school?'

'Yes.' She knew she would have to speak carefully now. It was not her place to pass comments, she knew, so she said: 'I'm sorry. I had no right—'

'Yes. I'm asking you now. I want to hear your opinion.'

'Then I'll tell you.' She was not aware of him pulling

into a layby at the side of the busy main road until the car halted, and he put on the handbrake.

'I – why have you stopped?'

'Because I want to hear what you have to say.'

'We – won't we be late?' she asked.

'No. Now tell me why the mention of boarding school shocked you.'

'All right. It's only my own opinion, though. It's this – Marie has never been used to other children's company, has she?'

'No.'

'Then it would be hard for her to adjust to being with others of her own age – a lot of them, all at once, as she would be if she was flung in at the deep end, as it were, in a boarding school. Not only that, but to leave home for the first time at the same moment – she – she would be very unhappy.'

'She's an intelligent child. She would adjust.'

'Would she? How do *you* know? Other children can be cruel, you know. She wouldn't know how to mix – not straightaway. She might adjust – but she might suffer first. I know, I was an only child – perhaps I was luckier than her, for I went to a small village school when I was young – she's always had a tutor.' Charlotte had forgotten that she was talking to the man she loathed, that she was on her way out with him – all that was in her mind was the desire to put across to him the importance of her feelings.

There was a brief silence. Then he spoke. 'You sound concerned about her welfare.'

'Concerned? Of *course* I'm concerned. I—' She stopped. She had nearly forgotten her promise to herself, not to argue with him *at all*. 'I – I'm very fond of Marie, although I've not known her for long. I can see something of myself in her, even though our circumstances are vastly different, of course.' There was no irony in her words. 'Basically every child is the same. They need security – and love.' She stopped, wondering if she had said too much.

'She has both those, surely?'

'Yes, I'm sure she has – I didn't mean—' she paused. What was the use? How could Jared possibly understand – a man like *him*? 'I've told you, it's really nothing to do with me, as a mere employee.'

He looked sharply at her, and she waited for the blast of anger that would surely come. Strangely enough, she no longer cared.

'Perhaps it has,' he said, in a mild tone. 'I'll think over what you said.' He wasn't angry!

She turned to look at him, utterly astonished, and he gave her a cool smile. 'You don't need to say it,' he said. 'You expected me to be annoyed, didn't you? I'm not. Because what you've just said only confirms something I'd already thought about. I'll try and work something out.' And he started the car and looked back to check the following traffic. In doing so he moved nearer to Charlotte, and she stiffened slightly, instinctively. Then they were roaring down the road, and the moment of brief tension passed.

But it left Charlotte in a state of confusion. She had thought him insensitive – he was not, not entirely anyway. She had thought herself immune to his nearness – she was not. She would, she decided, be glad when they arrived at their destination.

She had begun storing impressions the moment they arrived. Not only for Aunt Marie and Marie – but for Aunt Emily as well. The doorman who had ushered her from the car, dressed like something out of a musical set in Ruritania; the discreetly dressed swarthy men who had scrutinized their tickets before deciding they weren't gatecrashers; the opulent ladies' room, lavishly pink-curtained, with mirrors in which you could see yourself from all angles; the people. People who looked as if they spent their lives jetting round the world, who glowed with the kind of tans that took years to acquire, whose clothes were stunningly expensive, who just looked *different* from any she had met before.

And she was nervous, no use to try and hide it. Charlotte was unaware of the glances cast in her direction by others – unaware that in that hot-house setting, there was a clear fresh beauty about her that was equally distinctive, that her very shyness lent her an aura of fragility that could not but appeal to jaded palates.

There were several hundred people in the vast ballroom of the hotel, next to that the equally large restaurant had been converted so that there was a permanent running buffet attended by dozens of white-gloved waiters and waitresses. The orchestra was loud; it had to be to rise above the hundreds of voices all talking at once. Couples whirled around, men with trays of drinks skilfully avoided collisions as they threaded their way through a jostling, pushing throng; and Jared behaved with impeccable manners towards Charlotte.

She began to relax slightly. She was here at Madame Dupont's behest, and it wasn't turning out as bad as she had feared. In a way she could even begin to enjoy herself, simply by letting it wash over her, by imagining Jared was a polite stranger. They danced, and they spoke only of trivial things; he pointed out one or two celebrities, acknowledged the greetings of acquaintances, and Charlotte wondered why he couldn't always be like that.

And then it changed. He had gone away for a few minutes, asked her to excuse him, and she imagined that it was to talk to someone he had spoken to in passing only minutes before. He left Charlotte sitting on a gilt chair with a plate of smoked salmon by her side, a half full glass of champagne in her hand. 'I'll not be a minute,' he said. 'You don't mind?'

'No, of course not.' She wasn't alone, a couple of heavily jewelled matrons were a few seats along, tucking into caviare while they busily gossiped, and Charlotte took a sip of the bubbly liquid, and watched the couples whirling past, and a voice said:

'So there you are, all alone – that is terrible!' and a tall, very tanned, extremely attractive man sat beside her, and still speaking French, added: 'And your glass is nearly empty,' and he clicked finger and thumb, and a waiter with a full tray materialized from nowhere and bowed.

'There we are, thanks, Gaston,' he took two glasses, handed the bemused Charlotte one, took the other from her and downed it in a gulp, and handed the empty glass to the waiter who melted away again.

All Charlotte could think of to say was: 'Is his name Gaston?'

'Haven't a clue!' her companion confessed. 'But mine's Paul. You're English?'

'Yes. Does it show?'

'Considering that you stand out like a rose amid a load of tatty orchids – yes.' He had switched from French to very good English. 'And personally, if I were your escort, which sad to say I'm not, I wouldn't leave you alone for one second. How about a dance?'

'Oh, I don't think – he'll be back any second—' she looked round desperately. It was all too much like a certain party in Paris, and she didn't want to be reminded of *that*.

'Not him. He's busy talking to a crowd of Greek millionaires – I saw him leave you,' Paul said. 'He'll not get away for *ages*.' He stood up. 'Come on. It'll do him good.'

Why not? It would be something to tell Aunt Marie. *She* would appreciate it. Charlotte put her glass down. 'But the drinks—' she began.

'So?' He shrugged. 'They'll be there when – *if* – we come back,' and he held out his arms, and Charlotte, swallowing her last remnants of doubt, went into them.

Suddenly she saw Jared returning, but it was too late because Paul had quite a firm grip and was already skilfully whirling her into a crowd and ignored her protests. And Jared's eyes met hers across that short, rapidly growing distance, and she saw the expression she had most learned to dread – hard cold anger..

'Paul,' she said, 'my escort's back. I thought you said—'

'Did I? I must have been mistaken.' He looked down at her and laughed softly. 'You look terrified, my sweet. Now why should a gorgeous girl like you be frightened of a man like Jared de Marais—'

'You *know* him!' her eyes widened. 'I thought—'

'Who doesn't know him? It'll do him good to wait.'

He had said that before, just a few minutes previously. A tiny suspicion grew in Charlotte's mind – a suspicion that Paul was using her for reasons of his own because he didn't like Jared. Well, neither do I, she thought, but nobody is going to make me the scapegoat for their own personal quarrels.

'Why don't you like Jared?' she said abruptly. They were in the centre of the floor, where it was noisiest, and no one could possibly have overheard them.

He laughed, and his eyes gleamed. They were a very pale blue, a not unattractive colour, and his eyes were darkly lashed. 'Did I say that?'

'No. But it's fairly obvious.'

'Smart girl! You know, I like you. You never told me your name, by the way.'

'I don't want to now. I'm going back to Jared – will you please let me go?'

'I'll take you back if you're so anxious to see him. Come on.' Getting out from the milling bodies was more difficult than getting in. The world's most expensive perfumes assailed Charlotte's nose as they struggled through the crowd. She felt sick.

Jared was standing there, and close to, he looked even angrier than before. Angry – yet in a strange way very controlled.

'Evening, Jared.' Paul nodded. 'Enjoying yourself?'

'I was.'

'Were?' Paul grinned. 'Don't tell me I spoilt it for you?'

Jared was slightly taller than the other man, but they were built on the same lines. And Charlotte thought: They really hate one another.

'No, you didn't. It's getting a bore now, though. Thank you for looking after Charlotte for me. Your friends are looking for you.'

'Charlotte? You wouldn't tell me your name, would you?' He turned and smiled down at her. 'Now you've seen Jared, shall we continue our dance?'

Before she could answer, Jared said: 'I don't think so.'

'I was asking her, not you. Don't be tiresome, old boy, Charlotte can speak for herself.'

'But she doesn't know you. I do.'

142

Paul's eyes had turned to flint. 'Is that supposed to mean something?'

'You can take it how you like – old boy.'

Charlotte had had enough. The whole situation was beyond her, but they were both using her as a means to some curious ends of their own.

She bent to pick up the silver bag that Madame Dupont had lent to her, scooped the cobwebby lace stole from the back of the chair, looked at them both, and said, very coolly: 'Excuse me,' and walked away. She skirted the room, dodging couples, sidestepping to avoid waiters, her heart beating fast with fear and anger. Jared might be angry; she was equally so. She didn't know how much a taxi would cost to the villa, and had in any case had only brought a few francs with her, but she wasn't spending another moment with either of the men. They could sort out their battles without her assistance.

The Ruritanian doorman moved forward as she went down the steps. 'Madame requires a cab?' he inquired expressionlessly.

'Not – not yet, thank you.' She couldn't walk back to the villa, that was obvious, but she had to get away, if only to think, an impossibility with the hundreds of noisy people around her in the hotel. She moved briskly away from the brightly lit front of the building, then as it grew darker, her footsteps faltered. The night air was still warm, but she drew the stole round her shoulders and shivered slightly. Let Jared and Paul fight it out if they wanted to. For her the evening was over. She didn't care. She sat on a low wall, oblivious to the stares of passers by, until a *gendarme* stopped and spoke quietly.

'Is there anything wrong, *mademoiselle*?'

She looked up, forcing a smile. 'No – no, thank you,

I'm quite all right.'

'It is not advisable for Mademoiselle to be out alone so late.'

So late? 'What time is it?'

'Nearly twelve-thirty.' And as he spoke, she turned and saw Jared walking towards her. She stood quickly, and the policeman looked round in the direction of her glance and frowned.

'Charlotte, what the hell do you mean by running off?' he demanded, and the *gendarme* grinned broadly.

'*Ah, je m'excuse, mademoiselle*!'

'No, don't go,' Charlotte began, but Jared was there, and the dapper *gendarme* gave him a broad grin, a quick salute that spoke volumes.

Oh, but you don't understand, thought Charlotte bitterly. It's not a lovers' tiff, far from it – then Jared was beside her, face shadowed in the darkness of the night.

'Running off?' she retorted, her temper rising swiftly at the sight and angry sound of him. 'How *dare* you! Do you imagine you can use me as a – a – scapegoat in your pathetic little squabbles with your so-called friends?' As she moved away and he grasped her arm, she tried to shake it free.

'Get *off* me! Or I'll call that *gendarme* back!'

'No, you won't. Don't ever walk out on me like that again. No one does that.' He was still controlled, but less so.

'I just did!' she rejoined. 'And don't tell *me* what I can and can't do.'

'Listen,' he grated, 'this place isn't fit for a girl alone at night, it's as simple as that. I brought you here – you stay with me.'

'When you behave yourself I do – when you act like a

child I don't!'

'And how were you going to get back home?'

'To the villa? I hadn't decided. Probably by taxi.'

'But in the meantime you were sitting out here? Who were you hoping would come along – a fairy prince – or Paul?'

'Well, either would be preferable to *you*!' she shot back.

He laughed. 'You reckon? Paul eats little girls like you for breakfast.'

'I'm not standing here while you get rid of your temper on me,' she said. 'You should have had a punch-up with Paul – it's what you were both heading for. What happened – did you back down?' It was intended to sting him, and it succeeded.

'I wouldn't waste my time fighting – I'd have sorted him out with one hand tied behind my back.'

And Charlotte began to laugh. 'Oh, you should see your face! Just like a little boy bragging – ow! Let go of my arm!' She struggled, and he released her abruptly.

'We're getting the car. Come on,' he said grimly. She rubbed her arm and glared at him.

'Go to hell!'

'I'm going to count to five, and if you don't move I shall pick you up and *carry* you to the car. One – two—'

'You wouldn't dare!' she gasped, but he continued:

'Three – Four—'

'All *right*.' She moved away from him and towards the hotel. Because she knew then that he meant what he said.

A couple of notes changed hands, the doorman blew a whistle, and a few minutes later the Lamborghini glided to a halt in front of them, and a well-dressed youth got out, saluted, and handed Jared his keys.

She was helped into the car, and not a muscle had moved in that doorman's face. He could probably write a book about the things he had seen, she thought. Perhaps he had.

Jared roared away from the kerb, along streets still full of people, out of Cannes itself and along the main road towards the villa.

He had only done a mile or so when he swung abruptly from the main route and upwards on a smaller road. Charlotte looked back in puzzlement.

'This isn't the road home,' she said.

Jared ignored her, drove upwards, and the track grew narrower and more twisting, and it was all dark now, no more lights to guide them, only the headlamps sweeping through the impenetrable night. Then he pulled off the road, and switched off the engine and the headlamps, and it was pitch black, save for the dashboard gleam.

And Charlotte turned to him, suddenly frightened, saw the expression on his face, and took a deep breath.

'I'm not stopping here with you,' she breathed, and started to open the door. Silently he leaned across and clicked the lock.

'Oh yes, you are,' he said softly.

CHAPTER TEN

She went very still. There was nothing she could do, no way of escape from Jared. Yet strangely there was no fear in her. Perhaps she was past it; she no longer knew. She leaned back in the seat and realized she was utterly exhausted. Silence washed in all around them, broken by a click, the crackle of paper, then the rich aromatic scent of a cheroot filled the car, and she said: 'Why have you brought me here?'

'Because it's quiet, and because I don't fancy wandering round Cannes.'

'Why haven't you driven us back to the villa?'

'It's too early. We're not expected until two or three at the earliest.' His answers didn't make sense. She turned and looked sideways at him.

'I don't understand you.'

'Don't you? It's quite simple. We're staying here for another hour at least – and then we'll go.'

'You must be joking! Sit here for an hour? What will Aunt Marie think?'

'That we stayed until the end – or nearly – and that we had a pleasant evening.'

'Oh, really? She won't when I tell her what happened.'

'But you won't, will you? She's been ill – still is – and you're not going to upset her. She wants a full report – and you can give her one, can tell her what she wants to hear, and keep her happy.'

'You mean tell lies, don't you? Why don't you say it properly?'

'Because lies aren't necessary. You just omit to tell

her about Paul, that's all. There are enough other events to mention, I'm sure. And if all else fails, you can describe the food – she'll like that.'

Charlotte was silent. I'm damned if I'll just tamely do everything you tell me to, she thought. But she kept it to herself.

'So do you want to listen to the radio, or talk?' he added.

'I certainly don't want to talk to you,' she answered.

'No? Then we'll have some music instead.' And he switched on. Charlotte leaned back again, and went over the evening's events in her mind. The pictures were still vivid, the impressions too fresh and colourful to even try to sort out. But when morning came, she would, she knew that . . .

She opened her eyes because the car was moving. 'I thought you said we were stopping here,' she said, feeling very confused.

'I did, and we have – you've been asleep,' he answered dryly.

'I don't believe you,' she said.

'Look at your watch.'

She did. It was past two. 'I must have been tired,' she admitted.

'No doubt. At least you didn't have to make conversation with me,' he said, and did a rapid gear change that sent them speeding even faster along a nearly deserted highway.

Charlotte didn't speak. Because she was remembering her dream now. It came back to her clearly and in great detail, and with it a wave of disturbing emotion. For in that dream, Jared had kissed her, not once but several times, and not as it had been in the kitchen, but as it had been two years previously; warmly, affectionately –

148

beautifully. And her heart beat faster with the recollection, because something she had been trying to deny would no longer be denied. She had thought she hated Jared – had imagined that all the feelings for him had been erased by his brutal behaviour. But now she knew different. In spite of everything, she knew beyond a shadow of doubt that she still loved him. She turned slightly to look at him, to see his hard hawk-like profile as he drove along the road. What a fool I am, she thought. I should have been cured by now, seeing him with Margot, knowing how he regards me – how he despises me – but I'm not. And the knowledge was painful. Perhaps Aunt Marie knew. Charlotte closed her eyes. If so, let her be the only one, she prayed inwardly, let no one else see, for I couldn't bear it. She moved restlessly in her seat, and they started up the road to the villa, and Jared slowed down slightly and said: 'We'll have a drink when we get in.'

'Will we? So that you can brief me on what to say, and what not to say?' she retorted, her voice made sharper because of her efforts to hide the pain.

She saw his mouth tighten, saw his hands gripping the wheel, and she regretted her reply. Why rouse his anger unnecessarily? It did her no good.

'We've already been over that once. A drink will help you sleep, that's all.' His voice was calm.

'Oh. All right.'

He laughed. 'You're full of surprises. One minute spitting like a kitten, the next as cool as buttermilk.'

'Am I?' She bit on her tongue to hold back any more words, and he stopped the car, there, half-way along the drive, and turned to her.

'Yes, you are. Why the sudden changes?'

'Why the questions?' She felt breathless, because the last thing she wanted was this closeness, this intimacy –

not feeling as she did, bruised and vulnerable with the weight of her new knowledge.

'Because I want to know, that's why.'

'And supposing I don't w-want to tell you?' she ventured.

'I can't make you, can I?'

'Don't try.' Her voice came out as a whisper. Tension was mounting within her. In a moment, if he didn't drive on, she would get out of the car. And he moved, only slightly, but it was enough.

'No! Oh *no* – don't—' she fumbled desperately to open the locked door, heard his startled, half bitten-back oath, then strong fingers clamped down over hers, and he pulled her hand away from the lock.

'What the hell's the matter?' he twisted her round to face him. 'God, but I can't make you out at—'

'Let me *go*!'

'I'm not going to rape you, for heaven's sake – and I'm damned if I'm going hareing after you in the dark. You'll break a leg or something, you idiot. Now calm down and we'll get into the house. Don't worry,' he added grimly, 'I'll be glad to get rid of you.' And he started the engine as he spoke so that his words were nearly lost. Nearly, but not quite. Charlotte heard them, and closed her eyes. Of course he would. And it was at that moment that she knew she could not go on working for Madame Grenier for much longer. The image of Margot's cool beautiful face floated before her in the light from the headlamps. Margot. It was her he wanted. Yet how could she leave Marie? She couldn't do that either. Jared – Margot – Marie – the names repeated themselves endlessly in her tired brain, and Charlotte put her hand to her head to stop it spinning round.

The car stopped, but this time it was at the door. A

few lights shone out as if to welcome them home, but the bedrooms were in darkness. Jared closed his door quietly, came round to Charlotte's and opened hers.

'Gently does it,' he said. 'We mustn't wake the sleeping population,' and he put his hand under her arm to help her out. Charlotte didn't try and resist. There was only one person she could confide in, and perhaps in the morning, she would do so. Aunt Marie, because she, and only she, would understand.

Marie woke her at nine from a sound sleep. Charlotte opened her eyes to see the swim-suited girl sitting on the bed.

'Ah, you are awake – good!'

'With you bouncing up and down there's not much chance of rest,' Charlotte responded, still sleepily.

'Hah! Aunt Marie said I was not to wake you, so I thought, if I just sat here *quietly*,' Marie grinned impishly. 'I will ring for your breakfast now,' and she pressed the bell by the bed. Then seating herself, she said: 'Now, may I hear everything about your splendid evening? Jared has gone out – he is always dashing off somewhere, that one, but he told me before he went that he is taking us into Cannes this afternoon for a present for Aunt Marie.' She hugged her bare sunbrowned knees. 'Isn't that *lovely*?'

'Lovely,' agreed Charlotte, and struggled to sit up. 'What else did he tell you?'

'That you had spent a nice evening and met lots of interesting people.'

'Hmm, did he?' The more painful memories were returning now, and the knowledge that she still loved him – which had never really gone away – flooded back with an intensity that hurt. 'Yes, I suppose we did, though I don't remember all their names.' She began to

151

describe the hotel with its grand ballroom, the huge chandeliers that had glittered their golden lights on everyone, the women's dresses, the dazzling jewellery – words came easily, and the child listened, utterly fascinated, at the picture Charlotte painted.

In retrospect, she realized, it had been an experience not to be missed, something to remember for years and years – up until the moment when a man called Paul had spoken to her, and the evening had gone horribly awry. She must have hesitated, because Marie said impatiently: 'Yes? And then?'

'That's all for now. I want my breakfast, and anyway I'll be telling the whole story to your Aunt Marie later on.'

'All right.' There was a tap on the door, and Lucia came in. 'May I stay while you eat?'

'Of course.'

Later, as they sat out on the terrace, Charlotte repeated her vivid account of the evening. She described the food in minute detail, the impression made on her by the magnificently uniformed doorman, the discreet way their tickets were inspected, the wine, the dancing . . . everything in fact except the one incident that had caused the ball to come to an end for her – and for Jared.

She sensed that Madame Dupont was regarding her oddly once or twice, but it wasn't until Marie had at last scampered away to dive into the water that Charlotte found out why.

'So, you enjoyed your evening, did you?' the old woman asked with an innocent smile.

'Very much, thank you.'

'But you do not mention something that I would have thought even more fascinating than what you have already told us.'

Charlotte looked at her, puzzled, and Aunt Marie began to chuckle. 'Ah yes – I refer to Paul, of course.'

'Paul! But – did J-Jared tell you?'

'Him? Hah, certainly not *him* – no, I had a little phone call earlier this morning from a dear friend who wanted to tell me of the most interesting incident which occurred at the ball, when Jared and Paul had a slight difference of opinion—'

'Oh dear!'

'Oh dear, yes! Now come on, child, Marie is safely engaged in practising her Australian crawl – or something approaching it, and I am all agog, to put it mildly.'

Charlotte looked at her and gave a rueful smile. 'Jared practically forbade me to tell you. He said that as you'd been ill—' She was interrupted by a disbelieving snort, but went on: 'You shouldn't hear – but oh, I'm glad you asked. I need to tell someone, and I couldn't have a better person than you,' and she told the old woman exactly what had happened when Jared had left her alone for a few minutes.

When the story was done, Madame Dupont sighed. 'Ah, *quelle histoire*! And this Paul, you do not know who he is?'

'Only that he and Jared appear to dislike one another intensely.'

'Oh yes, that is true,' Aunt Marie's laugh rang out loud and clear. 'Ah, that I had been there! I will tell you about Paul. A very handsome man, is he not? And before Jared came on to the scene, he was Margot's constant escort – he is also the son of a man who was my dear late husband's greatest rival in business—'

But Charlotte had gone numb at the old woman's first words. So that was why! Humiliation washed over her, as she realized now the meaning for the bristling enmity between the two of them. Margot! She should have known! She closed her eyes to hide the pain from the other's shrewd gaze, and Aunt Marie said:

'But there is something else distressing you. Tell me.'

'I don't think I know how to begin,' Charlotte admitted.

'You do not? Then you must leave it. I have no wish to force anything out of you, my child.'

And Charlotte turned to her and said: 'It's just that – I don't think I can go on working for Madame Grenier for much longer. I thought my feelings for Jared were dead, but – but they're not.'

'Ah!' A long sigh. 'Love can be painful, *n'est-ce pas*? And men can be very blind. You poor girl. What are we to do with him?'

'Nothing. I shall have to sort it out for myself.' And she added quickly: 'I know you won't say anything—'

'Of course not! You will have to learn to be strong, Charlotte. It is the only way. Easy to say, difficult to do, I know. I too have had my heart broken in the past. But one recovers.'

'Yes, I know.' But when? she asked herself. How long do I have to wait before I'm cured – again? Not even the wise old woman would be able to answer that one.

'I think I'll have a swim with Marie, if I may.' Charlotte stood up and smoothed down her suit over her slender hips.

'Of course, of course. Away you go. Jared tells me that he will be in for lunch today. Please ring for Henri. I will have a little discussion with him about that, I think.'

Charlotte did so, then descended the steps into the glistening water. No diving today for her, her hair still felt too good from its careful dressing the previous evening. She intended it to last a while longer. She smiled wryly to herself for this small vanity, and had no idea just how beautiful she looked as she slid into the water. Nor had she any idea of what lay behind Madame Dupont's inscrutable expression as the old woman watched her go.

She and Marie laughed and played ball in the water for a while, and Charlotte could almost feel the sun tanning her as the wet droplets dried on her skin. She caught the ball and turned to Madame Dupont to make some remark about the heat, then caught her breath, because Jared was standing beside the old woman's seat, just watching her.

'Uncle Zhar!' Marie shrieked at the same moment. 'Go and get your trunks on and come in!'

'No,' he glanced at his watch. 'It's too near lunch now. Perhaps later. And you had better get dressed if you and Charlotte are coming out for a ride with me afterwards.'

'Oh yes! I forgot! Come on, Charlotte. We will let Uncle Zhar pull us out of the water. He is very strong, you know.' And Marie dived under and swam just below the surface to where Jared waited.

Charlotte saw his eyes rest on her arms as he pulled her up from the water, saw his slight frown, and looked in the direction of his glance. There was a large smudgy bruise just below her shoulder.

'Thank you,' she said, then to Aunt Marie: 'Marie and I will go and get changed.'

'Off you go.' Bright blue eyes had missed nothing, Charlotte felt sure. But she was equally sure that the old woman would say nothing. She still felt shaken from the brief encounter at the poolside when Jared had pulled her from the water – and just before that when she had looked up to see his eyes on her. The shock had been almost physical.

She chose a simple yellow dress that fitted her perfectly. But it was sleeveless, and she frowned as she looked in the mirror and saw the bruise. How – and then she realized. Jared had held her just there in their difference of opinion outside the hotel. Perhaps he too had remembered.

Aunt Marie remarked on it at lunch, and Charlotte said easily: 'I bumped my arm on a door,' and smiled, but her smile didn't reach Jared.

'Hmm, I see. Now, Jared, if you are taking the girls for a little ride – I wish I could come with you, but there, these doctors think they know best – I will give you a list of a few items I would like you to pick up for me in Cannes. You will do that?'

'With pleasure, Aunt Marie,' he answered.

'You are leaving for home on Sunday?' she asked, a little wistfully, it seemed to Charlotte.

'I'm afraid so,' he shrugged. 'Duty calls. You know how it is. I spoke to Aunt Heloise yesterday on the phone, and she seems to think we've all been away long enough. So—' he pulled a face, 'there it is.'

'But you will come again soon?'

'Of course.'

'And you, Charlotte, you will come too?' The old woman turned to Charlotte, who nodded.

'Of course – if I am asked.' And if I'm still there, she thought.

'Then that is settled. And if Heloise needs reassurance, I will have to be "poorly" again, won't I?'

Jared laughed. 'You could get away with murder, and you know it, Aunt. Anyway, what's to stop you coming up to visit us? I'll even come and fetch you if you want.'

'You will? Hmm, now *there's* a thought.' The old woman's eyes brightened, and Charlotte thought: I bet she will too. 'Of course, I'll have to get a little better first – but it would be something to look forward to.'

'Then we will make arrangements now. You *will* be better by the time of the harvesting of the grapes. Think of the parties – think what a time you will have, Aunt Marie. All you have to do is obey the doctors and – *voilà!*'

'I am tempted.' Aunt Marie pushed away a piece of crusty bread that Marie had offered her. 'No child, *rien plus de pain* – I will start on that diet this *minute!*' And her hearty laugh shook the wine glasses on the table, and so infectious was it that they all joined in.

The road was long, and Jared's driving assured as he took them in the Lamborghini to Cannes later that day. He parked behind a hotel where he was obviously well known, for there was a whispered consultation with an attendant and notes changed hands. He caught up with Charlotte as she followed Marie out towards the promenade.

'Did I make that bruise?' he asked quietly.

Charlotte looked at him. 'It wasn't anybody else,' she said. 'But don't apologize – I wouldn't expect it of you.'

'Then I won't. It wouldn't do to spoil my image, would it?' he answered easily.

To think that I love you, she thought. I must be mad. 'Where are we going?'

'It all depends what kind of present you want. Marie seems to be heading for one of those outrageously expensive girls' shops. Hey, Marie, wait!' he called.

The girl halted and turned, eyes alight with happiness. At least one person is enjoying herself, Charlotte reflected.

'What are you going to buy for Aunt Marie?' he

demanded.

'A vase or a statue or something. Why?'

'I just wondered. I know a shop which might just do—' and he paused deliberately, smiling.

She jumped up and grabbed his hand. 'All right. Where? Let's go now.'

'Patience, child, patience. There's plenty of time. It's too hot to rush. Now, follow me.'

The streets were crowded, the tall buildings elegant and beautiful, shimmering in the sun, and beyond that the green Mediterranean beckoned them, with its moored yachts bobbing gently in the harbour. In the distance a water-skier cut a white foamy path across the water, and gulls cried their sad cries, and Charlotte gazed about her in wonder. This was the paradise of the very rich, and she was staying here in a villa that was the ultimate in luxury. A situation she could not have believed possible only weeks before.

And what was it Aunt Emily had said? 'I have a feeling that this job is for you.' In one way her hunch – her womanly intuition, had been right – in another, sadly awry. For who could have foreseen Jared?

Charlotte bit her lip. She would have to tell her soon.

'Mind the traffic.' The voice of the man in her thoughts jerked her back to the present from her momentary daydream. His hand on her arm was warm and restraining, and she saw the shirt-sleeved, white-gloved *gendarme* directing the traffic at a busy junction, and they waited to cross with the colourfully dressed throng. A hand waved, traffic screeched, feet marched across, and Marie held tightly to Jared's hand and said:

'I'm thirsty.'

'You want a drink now?'

'Yes, please, Uncle Zhar.' She had seen the pavement

café before they had.

'All right. Charlotte, what will you have?'

'Lemonade – anything cold, please.'

They sat at a red metal-topped table shaded by a huge umbrella emblazoned with the word 'Martini' repeated all round it. A handsome young waiter brought them their drinks on tiny saucers, and Marie sighed luxuriously.

'This is *lovely*!' she said. 'I do like coming out with you, Uncle Zhar – and Charlotte, of course,' and she smiled at Charlotte reassuringly. 'I mean, it's so *nice* to be with my favourite people. What a pity Aunt Marie couldn't come as well. Do you think she will come and visit us?'

'I'm sure she will,' he answered. Charlotte sipped her icy fizzy drink and watched him. In open-necked blue sports shirt he looked strong and attractive, a deeply tanned man, seemingly unaware of the lingering glances of passing women. 'But first she must get better. Then I will come and fetch her, as I promised.'

'And can Charlotte and I come too?' the girl asked. Oh, please, thought Charlotte, please don't go on. You don't know what you're doing.

'I'd need a bigger car, wouldn't I?' he asked. 'There's only room for us—'

'But you could come in the Daimler,' she interrupted. 'See, *that* is big enough for *lots* of people—'

'Drink up, chatterbox. No wonder you're so thirsty. You never stop talking!'

Marie laughed. 'You are funny. You try and sound cross, but I know you're not. I can tell by your face. All those little laughter lines round your eyes disappear when you are angry. But they are still there.'

'All right, Sherlock Holmes. Drink up, and if you're so clever *you* can take us to the shop.'

'What is it called?'

'Cobwebs.'

'Cobwebs—' Clearly the girl was puzzled. 'I don't know the word.'

'And I thought you knew everything! *Les toiles des araignées* in French, okay? And before you ask, it is called that because it belongs to an English friend of mine, and it's full of antiques and all sorts of interesting things, and it's in the next street – so you can lead the way and find it for us.'

'All right.' Marie finished her drink and stood up. 'I'm ready.'

'Are you ready, Charlotte?' he asked politely.

She stood up. 'Yes. Thank you for the drink.'

'A pleasure.' The smile he gave her was for Marie's benefit, not hers, she knew that. A helpless sensation swept over her. A feeling of frustrated anger, and no way to escape it. As long as she stayed working for Madame Grenier she must suffer it whenever he was near. She looked directly at him and met the challenge of his gaze with her own clear blue eyes. Why *should* I suffer? she thought suddenly. Why the hell should I? I've had enough from you, taken all I can stand. I'm going to start fighting back now. And something must have communicated itself to him, for she saw the hardening of his face – and she smiled slowly at him. All in the space of a few seconds it had happened – Marie was a few yards away, fascinated by the antics of a small boy with his parents, oblivious to them – and in those few moments Charlotte had been possessed by a new resolve, perhaps triggered off by Madame Dupont's words – 'You will have to learn to be strong, Charlotte' —

'Marie isn't watching you,' she said quietly. 'You don't need to put on the act for *me*.'

'What do you mean?' Calm, not aggressive – yet.

She lifted one eyebrow. 'I don't have to tell you – for you already know. But you can't bother me any more – I don't *care*.' And she turned away to follow Marie, and left him waiting by the chairs. It was like a warm glow inside her. Somehow she had found the strength. She would not let him hurt her any more. When they returned to the villa she would tell Aunt Marie so.

CHAPTER ELEVEN

SHE knew she was different now. It was as though she had succeeded in building a wall around her heart. It might ache inside, but he would never know. No one would. And as they walked along baking pavements she remembered the look she had seen on his face, just for an instant, when she had come down the stairs at the villa the previous evening. She had known then the dizzy sense of power possessed by a beautiful woman. Just for a second, but if it could happen once, it could do so again. It's all in the mind, she thought in wonder. If I tell myself that I'm beautiful, I will be – and if I tell myself I'm full of confidence, then that will also be so. She took a deep breath and held her head high. Would Aunt Marie understand? Somehow Charlotte knew that she would. There would be much to talk about at the villa when they returned.

Marie skipped ahead, reading the signs above the shops, hesitating, frowning, then going on. Then she stopped and pointed. 'Look, Uncle Zhar,' she called. 'We are here!'

'Right!' he held up his hand in acknowledgment. He was walking beside Charlotte, had been since he'd caught her up after their drink. They hadn't spoken; there was nothing to say. But the air was charged with brittle tension – only now Charlotte, instead of feeling frightened by it, was enjoying it. For he was puzzled she knew that as surely as if he had told her. Good, she thought. 'I hope this shop isn't too pricey,' she remarked as they neared it, 'these sort of places usually are.'

'Don't worry, I know James too well.'

'How nice for you,' she murmured, almost as if to herself, then smiled as he glanced at her quickly.

She paused outside the window, to which Marie had her nose glued. Her heart sank slightly. And hopes of a dusty antique shop crammed with bargains vanished in an instant as she looked inside. Pictures, ornaments, vases and jewellery were there all right, cleverly arranged to tempt the passer-by – and not a price ticket to be seen – which was probably just as well, she thought. It was certainly not a place she would venture in alone, for every item in the window had the stamp of quality and luxury about it. Rich dark green velvet was the backcloth on which everything was placed. Larger pictures at the back, figurines at the centre, a few rings scattered, seemingly casually, in the foreground, heavy antique rings that glowed with beauty and colour.

Marie pointed to a small figure of a girl holding a basket of fruit. 'I like *that*,' she announced. 'Will you ask your friend how much it is?'

'You have undoubted good taste, my child,' he grinned. 'That's Capo di Monte and probably costs a fortune. However, we'll go in and see, shall we?' He held out his hand to usher them in.

The interior was cool, and they were surrounded by antique writing desks, chairs, bookcases full of old books, picture-covered walls, a row of grandfather clocks ... Charlotte looked around her in quiet wonder. What a splendid place to browse uninterrupted. How Aunt Emily would love it!

'Jared! Come on in. You're a stranger, how are you?' The voice came from the back of the shop, and then a man came forward to shake Jared's hand. Probably in his early forties, he was dark and smiling, stockily built, with a black bushy beard obscuring most of his face. His eyes were friendly enough – and shrewd. He looked at Charlotte and grinned, then at Marie. 'And friends too. Welcome, all of you.'

'Charlotte, I'd like you to meet James Walker, an old friend of mine – James, Charlotte Lawson and my niece Marie. We're staying at my aunt's place for a few more days,' he said as they shook hands.

'How is Madame Dupont? I've not seen her for ages.'

'Not too bad at present. Why don't you go and visit her some time? She'd be glad to see you. It's her birthday tomorrow, which is why we're here.'

'Ah!' James nodded. 'Thought you'd have a good reason for coming. Well, this is the right place, old boy. I'll look after you.'

Jared smiled. 'Take us for a ride, you mean.'

James' face expressed great pain. 'You wound me. And in front of ladies! How could you?'

'Because I know you.'

'Hmm, you have a point. However, it's bargain day today. Now,' this more briskly, 'what have you got your eye on?'

James winced. 'Capo di Monte? Clever child,' he grinned at Marie.

He looks like a sea captain, thought Charlotte, not an antique shop proprietor. But he seems nice – I wonder what he's doing being a friend of Jared's?

He lifted the figure out carefully. It was exquisite, a miniature of a girl who looked in a way like Marie herself. The little girl took a deep breath. 'How much is it, please? I have my purse.'

Jared raised a finger. 'Can I just have a quick word in your ear, James – won't take a moment?'

James put the figure carefully down on a rosewood table. 'Look at it, Marie,' he said. 'But if you pick it up, do so very gently.' He vanished with Jared to the back of the shop. Charlotte thought she knew why they had gone. Well, that was fair enough. He had more money than he knew what to do with, and doubtless Marie's pocket money was rationed.

They were only away a couple of minutes, and neither face gave anything away when they returned. James clapped his hands briskly together.

'Where were we?' he asked. 'Ah yes, you wanted to know the price of that charming piece, didn't you, *mademoiselle*?' Then he said it, and Charlotte kept her smile to herself. A quick mental calculation to translate francs to pounds, and it was obvious what arrangements Jared had come to with his friend. He was almost giving it away.

'Then may I have it? I have enough,' Marie almost gasped in delight.

'You certainly may. We'll find a box and some packing, shall we?'

Jared spoke. 'You aren't looking round, Charlotte.'

'No,' she smiled. 'I don't think—'

'Try, you never know. Hey, James, anything interesting for Aunt Marie?'

The voice came from the back recesses of the shop where James and Marie were clearing searching for something, judging by the sound of drawers opening and closing. 'Some odds and ends in a box at your left. Try it. I know Madame Dupont likes chunky jewellery.'

Jared lifted down a heavy old box and opened it. Charlotte took a deep breath at the sight of the treasures within – bracelets, rings, necklaces, pendants – everything jumbled up as though poured in willy-nilly.

'That's some new stuff I haven't sorted through yet,' James' voice called. 'It'll want cleaning too, but I can do that in a jiffy.'

Charlotte knew she wouldn't be able to afford anything, but the temptation to handle such beautiful jewellery was too strong to resist. She lifted out a heavy gold ring with a deep red stone and slipped it on her finger and sighed. 'Beautiful!' she whispered. Jared didn't attempt to touch anything. He just stood there, watching, waiting. Only now Charlotte didn't care. She rifled through the rest, carefully untangling a fine silver chain before lifting out the pendant that it held and resting it in the palm of her hand. It was small and quite simple, a stone of blue shading to mauve. She put it out on the table beside the box and dug in again, this time to bring out a gold chain bracelet fastened with a tiny padlock. No, that was plain and heavy. She didn't even like it. Her eyes were dazzled with the colour and sheer variety of it all. And each item told a story, each was old, that was sure.

'Seen anything you fancy?' Jared's voice was almost an intrusion.

She looked up at him. 'Nearly all of it – but you don't need to tell me it'll be dear.'

'That pendant – why have you left it out?'

She picked it up. 'I like the stone, I'd like to ask your friend how much it would be.'

'How much is this pendant, James?' Jared called. 'It's got a stone that looks like an amethyst.'

'A what? Hang on.' James bustled out and picked it up. 'Hmm, that one – I don't know how that got there – oh, you can have it for a couple of quid – do you want it, Jared?'

'Charlotte might. Well, Charlotte?'

Two pounds! She looked from it to James, who seemed frankly disinterested, and back again to the pendant.

'I'll have it,' she said. And she still didn't realize. Not until later, and then it was too late.

Jared chose a picture that Charlotte had noticed on entering the shop, and liked, a landscape that might have been a Constable but obviously wasn't, but was very pleasant and restful to look at. He didn't even ask the price, just told James he would take it.

'Right. Now you'll come in the back for coffee before you go?'

Jared looked at Charlotte. 'Charlotte? Would you like a coffee?'

'Oh yes, thank you very much,' she smiled at James.

It wasn't until she had begun her coffee that she realized she still wore the ring with the red stone. Putting down her cup, she said faintly: 'I'm sorry, I put this ring on to try it before – and forgot I had it on.'

Marie laughed. 'Wouldn't it be funny if you couldn't get it off? Then you'd have to buy it!'

But Charlotte had already taken the ring from her finger, and put it on the table beside her. In a way, the room in which they were sitting was an extension of the shop, full of antique furniture and heavy lamps and statues. But it was all arranged in such a way that they sat comfortably, Charlotte and Marie on a purple velvet-upholstered chaise-longue, the two men on hard-backed dining chairs. 'Shall I put it back in the box?' she volunteered.

'No,' James shook his head. 'Enjoy your drink. Have another biscuit?'

Marie was the only one who wanted one, and they stayed for a while longer before Jared looked at his watch and remarked that they really ought to go if Aunt Marie wasn't to send out search parties for them, which amused Marie greatly. Both girls paid for and received their gifts, and Jared stayed behind as they walked out.

He caught them up as they were half-way down the street. He carried the wrapped picture under one arm. But that hadn't been the reason for his staying. He had waited for them to go before paying for the picture, and the extra for Marie's statuette, and . . . And it was then that Charlotte saw what she should have seen half an hour before when she had asked the price of the pendant. What a fool she had been! What a *stupid* idiot. She stopped walking and looked down at the two small packages she carried, her own and Marie's. Jared paused, looked back, and she glanced up – and the expression on his face told her what she needed to confirm her deep suspicions. But she said nothing. She merely met his look with her own. Her new-found confidence was still too fragile to risk challenging him now. Later, she would. Later, when she had planned what to say, and *how* to say it.

'Anything the matter?' he asked.

'Nothing – nothing at all. Should there be? The presents are delightful, aren't they? I'm sure Aunt Marie will be very pleased.' And she smiled innocently at him and walked on. That was two evening dresses, and now the difference in price of a pendant. One day soon she would pay him back every penny of the money. Busily planning how to save it up, she walked quickly along. When she left the château, as she eventually would, she would be in his debt for nothing.

They watched films that evening at the villa – not on television, but on a large screen fitted up in the lounge. Nothing surprised Charlotte any more; she wouldn't have been astonished if an usherette had appeared with ice creams in the interval between the cartoons and the main film, but it was Lucia who came in with champagne instead. Madame Dupont was comfortably ensconced on a settee, Charlotte and Marie by her side on another settee, Jared slightly behind them on a chair. Henri operated the projector, and with the faint blue smoke wreathing round them from Jared's cigar, the atmosphere was almost that of a real cinema.

It was an American western – these were Aunt Marie's favourites, as she told Charlotte while they sipped their champagne before the start, and it was funny to hear James Garner speaking perfect French even though she knew it was dubbed. She was very aware of Jared behind her, although he didn't speak. She had had no chance to speak to Aunt Marie alone since their return from Cannes, and any conversation had been general. They had called at a shop to collect some flowers that Madame Dupont had ordered before they returned to the villa, and had each bought a birthday card from the shop adjoining it. The only problem Charlotte had had since returning was preventing Marie from blurting out about the presents. And now it was late, and Marie would soon be in bed, and tomorrow they would be giving them anyway.

The film over, the screen rolled away by Henri, Marie looked at Charlotte.

'Shall I go to bed now?' she asked her.

'I think it would be a good idea,' Charlotte answered, and winked at the girl, who stood and went over to kiss Aunt Marie.

'Oh, you're going to have a marvellous birthday tomorrow,' she whispered as she hugged her.

'Am I?' The old woman chuckled. 'Good. Off you go, *ma petite*. Sleep well.'

Then Jared stood up. 'I'm away myself, Aunt Marie. Shall I help you upstairs before I go?'

'No, Henri will do that. Are you deserting me too, Charlotte?'

Charlotte shook her head. 'Not if you'd like me to stay. I'm not tired.'

'Good. We will have a drink as well. Good night, Jared.'

'Good night, Aunt Marie,' he bent to kiss her forehead. 'Good night, Charlotte,' very formally.

She turned and smiled at him. 'Good night,' very brightly.

Aunt Marie let out her breath in a deep sigh when he had gone. 'There are drinks in that corner cupboard, child,' she said. 'We won't bother Henri. Now, what have you to tell me?'

Charlotte couldn't stop the laughter that bubbled out. 'How – how do you know I have anything to tell you?' she asked.

'Ah! I've been watching you! And Jared is one very puzzled man. And you – *you* have a certain air about you that is difficult to describe. So what is it?'

'I think it's something you said, as a matter of fact,' Charlotte began, after she had poured them both a glass of wine on Madame Dupont's instructions. 'And we had just finished a drink at a pavement café in Cannes, and I looked at him and thought – why the hell should I let *you* upset me? – and something clicked, as I remembered your words about being strong – and I told him that nothing he could do would bother me any more, then I walked off and left him standing there.' She remembered the scene vividly, the expression on his face, and was filled with remorse. 'Oh, was I terrible?'

'Terrible? You? No! I would have liked to see that! Perhaps that is the first time anyone has treated him thus. Good for you, Charlotte. I love Jared dearly, as I'm sure you know, but I am well aware that he is arrogant at times – he's a very strong character – and likes his own way, which is only like most men, I suppose. It will do him good. But do you think you can keep it up? You mustn't weaken once you have started.'

'I know – oh, Aunt Marie, it is awful to feel like this about anyone, isn't it? And it's awful for me to be talking about him like this, I know that too. I am an employee of his aunt – and you are their very good friend, and I—'

'And you are a young woman who has been badly treated by him. Do not forget *that*, my child. This in a way has nothing to do with the fact of your employment. You are doing your task well with Marie, I know that. You are a person, and we are all important – remember that. You are doing the right thing – remember that too. So now I know why he is so mystified – you see, I was aware of the difference in your manner. It suits you!' Seeing Charlotte's expression of concern, she added: 'Yes, it does, truly! Don't let *me* down.'

'All right, I won't. Oh!' Charlotte sighed. 'Wouldn't it be nice if you were at the château – I could come to you when I needed advice.'

'You can write to me or phone me if you feel the need to talk. I am always here – and I understand, perhaps as no one else could, my dear. For I know Jared very well – and I feel I am beginning to know you too – in many ways I am reminded of myself when young every time I look at you.' She nodded. 'Oh yes, don't look surprised, it is quite true. One is very unsure of oneself when young – ah, to have the knowledge at twenty that one has at forty! But you are learning fast.'

'You make me feel better,' Charlotte confessed. 'Much better – about everything.'

'Fine. Drink up your wine. A drop more?'

'No, thanks, or I'll have a hangover in the morning –

and I want to be wide awake to enjoy your birthday.'

'Then I won't bother either. I too need to be fresh, for I have a feeling I may be woken early by Marie with some little surprise.'

'I think you will,' Charlotte agreed.

'There will be a few old friends in to dinner – just two or three. Will you wear that dress?'

'Of course, if I may.'

'It is yours now, don't forget that. You are to take it with you when you go. I couldn't be more pleased. What use is it hidden away in an old wardrobe? My grand-daughter's scorn it for the more modern clothes – they do not realize, as you and I do, just how very feminine the older-fashioned dresses can be.'

'Thank you very much for it, Aunt Marie.'

'And now, I think it is bedtime. Will you ring for Henri?'

It was not Marie who woke Charlotte, but the insistent ringing of the front door bell at the villa. She heard voices, then the sound of movement, as if something heavy was being carried in. She found out what it had been when, washed and dressed a short time afterwards, she went out of her room to go downstairs. The hall was filled with masses of beautiful flowers arranged in tall baskets, dozens and dozens of them. For a moment she stood there just looking, astonished beyond words, and Jared's voice came from behind her: 'Good morning.'

She turned to him. 'Good morning. I was looking at that gorgeous display.'

'Yes. Aunt Marie likes flowers. She's living in the right place for them too. Are you going down to break-fast?'

'Yes.' She didn't wait to see if he was, just started walking down, slowly, calmly. It was all too easy now –

but would it be the same when they were back at the château? That was something no one could answer. One thing was sure – she would soon find out.

Aunt Marie was already up, walking slowly to greet them as they reached the dining-room. Clad in a long white dress with batwing sleeves, she held up her hands in welcome.

'Good morning, my dears. Marie woke me at crack of dawn with the most exquisite present, so I had to get up to make the most of my day!'

Charlotte went forward and kissed the old woman's cheek. 'Happy birthday, Aunt Marie,' and she handed her the wrapped gift.

'Oh, come, I must sit down and open it.' She embraced Jared, who wished her a happy birthday and then added:

'I'll go and get my present. I didn't think you'd be up yet. Excuse me.'

'What a lovely pendant! Oh, I shall wear it now. Carefully, Charlotte, mind my hair!' The deep chuckle rose from her throat as Charlotte slipped the chain over her head as the old woman sat in a chair in the dining-room. 'Marie is out picking me some roses from the garden – there, that looks lovely. Thank you, Charlotte – but you shouldn't have spent all that money, you know—'

No, thought Charlotte, that's the one thing I could hardly tell you, but dear Jared will be paid back, every franc.

It seemed as if the doorbell never stopped ringing all morning, with cards and gifts galore arriving by messengers and postmen. The sun shone brightly from a cloudless sky as they sat on the terrace by the pool, and the extension phone shrilled constantly by Aunt Marie's side. Charlotte lay and sunbathed while Marie swam with Jared in the pool. There was ample time to think. What would the dinner be like that evening? Would it only be two or three old friends for dinner, as Aunt Marie had assured her? Or would there be a crowd? Mentally, she went over all the make-up tips the older woman had taught her before the disastrous evening out on Wednesday. They were all clear in her mind. She resolved to look her very best. In a way it would be an important test, she felt sure, although she didn't know quite why.

'Mmm, yes, Charlotte, you can put more eye-shadow on, you haven't got quite enough,' Marie said, frowning thoughtfully, clearly taking over where Aunt Marie had left off.

'Thank you,' Charlotte answered, and carefully shaded more of the silver-grey powder above her eyes. She was taking her time, not rushing at all, and actually enjoying it. I'm getting a conceited hussy, she thought wryly. At one time I would have scorned this performance, but it's a challenge now. And in a way, it's all due to Jared – although that's something he'll never know.

'Is that better?' she asked her critical watcher at last.

'Oh yes, you look simply beautiful, Charlotte. I hope *I'll* be beautiful when I'm grown up.'

'Of course you will!' Charlotte smiled at her warmly. 'And now, are we ready?' She eased off the towel she had put round her shoulders while she made up, and moved from the stool. The dress glowed warmly on her, complimenting her golden skin and hair, giving her the appearance of a fairy-tale princess – but she knew only that she felt good, and that would suffice.

Marie had a long dress on, pale blue with small flowers. Charlotte had brushed the child's hair until it shone, and her cheeks glowed rosy red. 'You look extremely pretty,' she told her. 'Let's go down and greet Aunt Marie's friends.' Together they left the room.

It was late. The dinner was over, the night was so warm that they had all drifted out on to the patio, and Charlotte, standing quietly beside Marie, looked round her, treasuring the scene, knowing that this was something she would remember for the rest of her life. The meal had been superb, but more important, the people, Aunt Marie's friends, were delightful. The 'one or two' had turned out to be eight, so that twelve people had sat down to eat at nine o'clock, and since that time, nearly three hours previously, the talk had flowed as freely as the wine. Aunt Marie was the centre of it all, no doubt about that, and enjoying every moment of her own day. And now she was calling something to Jared, who stopped talking to a couple near to Charlotte and Marie and answered his aunt.

'But I insist!' she shouted, and Charlotte began to listen. There was a general burst of laughter, a rising murmur of voices, and the man nearest Charlotte, an elderly doctor, said: 'It seems as if Jared has no choice.'

'I didn't hear—' she began, smiling, and Marie pulled her hand and said loudly:

'Aunt Marie wants Jared to play the guitar!'

'Oh.'

The man, Dr. Roche, smiled at them both. 'You have not heard him before?'

'No,' Charlotte admitted. She didn't particularly want to, but she thought it more tactful not to add that.

'Ah, then you will have a pleasant surprise. And if we are lucky, no doubt Madame Dupont will sing for us.'

She really shouldn't feel so amazed, she knew that. She should have got used to the constant state of bewilderment by now. So many things, in so few weeks . . .

'Madame Dupont sings?' she asked faintly.

'But yes! You will see.'

The lights blazed out from the house on to the terrace, and moths fluttered round their heads, and the air was sweet with the scent of flowers, and everyone drifted to the chairs set beside the pool, and sat down.

'Come,' Dr. Roche touched Charlotte's arm. 'Sit down here, and you too, Marie.'

Jared had vanished through the french windows, and the murmur of voices began again, and Charlotte and Marie obeyed the doctor, who then sat beside them. Henri moved discreetly among them, distributing more champagne, removing empty glasses, quiet as ever.

Charlotte found herself waiting for Jared to return, and in spite of everything, a small, unwilling excitement grew within her – a sense of anticipation that she didn't quite understand.

And then he was there, and pulling a chair up beside a table, so that he could sit on the table and rest one foot on the seat. 'Talk among yourselves,' he called. 'I've got to tune this damned thing.' A burst of laughter followed his words, and Charlotte watching him, thought: Everyone likes him, you can tell. It showed before and during dinner, and he was amusing and courteous to everyone – including Charlotte – only once she had found him looking at her before he could glance away, and her breath had caught in her throat, because there was something in that look . . . Only for a moment, then it was gone, but she remembered it now and she watched him as with bent head he tuned the instrument. Long fingers caressed the strings, he listened intently, then looked up.

'All right. What's it be be?' he called. 'Aunt Marie, it's your party. What shall I play?'

'You know my favourite – *Mes Jeunes Années*.' There was a quiet murmur of approval, and Charlotte puzzled over what the song could be, for she didn't recognize the title. Then he began to play – and a shiver of excitement ran up her spine as she recognized the tune – and heard words that she remembered only too well. She had to sit still, had to deliberately force herself from moving away, for the last time she had heard it had been at the fateful party in Paris when she and Jared had met. They had danced to it, and then the words had held a special magic, because it was a magical night – and now he was singing it, and something tore at her heart and made her want to cry out, to tell him to stop . . .

'Dreams never grow old, they shine through the years.' . . . That record at the party had been sung by Les Compagnons de la Chanson, in English, and Jared was singing it in French, but the words were the same, and their message was eternal.

His voice was pleasant, and all except his were stilled, with not even a glass chinking. Applause flooded the terrace when he had done, and then Aunt Marie sang another song, and everyone joined in a third, and Charlotte gradually relaxed. He hadn't done it deliberately, because Aunt Marie had requested it, and in any case he would have forgotten. Charlotte hadn't, but she knew he had, for what was one party to him, amongst so many?

But then he sang it again, and she wasn't so sure. Because, as he began it, he looked across at Charlotte, and it seemed as if his eyes mocked her. She couldn't stand it any more. 'Excuse me,' she whispered to the doctor, who sat with eyes closed, listening, enjoying himself. She passed him and quickly, quietly, walked into the house. No one noticed. They were all too enraptured with the sweet soft sound of the guitar being played.

Charlotte ran up to her room. Tears filled her eyes. Blinking furiously, she dabbed with a handkerchief, careful not to smudge the mascara she had so recently applied, trembling with an inner sadness that was almost overwhelming. She didn't want to go down again – but she would have to, if only to be with Marie, for it was late. But at least not until the song was done, for it was unbearable. She sat on the bed. Through the open window she could hear the faint strains of the music in its closing bars. Then it was over, and they were clapping, and then laughing, and she wondered vaguely why, but she didn't care any more. She looked ceilingwards, not really seeing anything, only wondering how soon the pain would disappear completely.

It was time to go now. Before anyone commented on her disappearance. She opened the door, and Jared was coming along the corridor. She shut it again – too quickly, and heard his voice:

'Charlotte?'

'No,' she whispered. 'Oh no, go away,' but too quietly for him to hear.

Then he was opening the door, coming in, and she looked at him, too shocked to speak. There was a very strange expression on his face.

CHAPTER TWELVE

CHARLOTTE found her voice. 'What do you want?' she asked.

'Why did you disappear?' he asked, and his voice had a quality to it that made her go warm. He stood there in front of her, and he had never seemed so tough and powerful as he was now. Charlotte was frightened. Easy to be confident in daylight, easy to talk about it with Aunt Marie, and receive good advice, but her nerves were raw, her whole body still shaking from the effect of hearing a song that had brought back too many memories, far too many . . .

'Do I – do I have to explain all my moves to you?' she asked, and prayed for courage, because he was shutting the door, and the handle clicked with a note of finality that made her nervous. It was as if he didn't intend to leave . . . .

'No. But I was watching you. It was the song, wasn't it?'

She looked up at him then, eyes widening. 'You knew – you *knew*?'

'Yes, I knew.' There was something wrong. His aggression was gone, he stood there in front of her, and the tawny gold eyes held an expression she had thought she would never see again. Her heart beat faster, and then she turned, so that she didn't have to face him, so that he wouldn't see . . .

'Please go away,' she said. 'Please leave me alone.'

'No,' he said. 'It's no use, Charlotte.' He put his hand out, and touched her arm, and his touch was of fire, but she made no attempt to shake him off. She doubted if she had the strength. Instead she stood very still. *Very* still. Tension throbbed in the air they breathed, and the light shimmered on the mirror casting rainbow-coloured darts of light from its surface, and she took a deep shuddering breath, and Jared reached out his other hand and pulled her gently round to face him, and for a second he looked down at her. Then with infinite gentleness, he bent his head to kiss her.

Charlotte didn't struggle. She no longer knew how to. Her face was upturned, and his lips were warm and tender, and this kiss was like no other she had ever known in her life, and it went on for ever and ever . . .

Jared looked down at her again, and there was such a great agony on his face that she gasped, and instinctively put up her hand to touch his cheek.

'Why, Jared, what is it?' she whispered. He turned his face towards her hand, to rub his mouth against her palm, and voice husky, answered:

'It's no use fighting it any longer, Charlotte. I've tried to hate you, to put you out of my life – but I can't. If Aunt Marie hadn't asked me to play that song, I would have done so anyway. Because I wanted – I *needed* to know something. And I think I do.'

'What do you know?' It was unbelievable. She was in his arms, but she wasn't trying to get away because she didn't want to.

'I think I know that – you don't hate me either.' She could barely hear the words.

'I tried to – oh, how I tried!' And now she had strength enough to move free, and did so. She could see him more clearly that way. 'When you greeted me that first time at – at – the *château*—' her voice faltered as the memories came back, 'I felt so unhappy, I—'

'Don't, Charlotte. Please don't—' he moved as there

came a sound from outside, and Marie's voice calling:

'Charlotte? Uncle Zhar? Where are you?'

With a muttered oath he went to the door and opened it.

'Yes, Marie, what do you want?'

'I want Charlotte to hear me play too—' so that was the reason for the laughter, '—and I thought you'd come to fetch her.'

'Yes, yes, I had.' He looked round at Charlotte. In his eyes there was a plea. But for her the spell was broken. What madness had possessed her – and him? She didn't know.

'I'll come now,' she answered. 'I was just coming anyway.' There was a lump in her throat.

'Wait, Charlotte—' he began, but she ignored it, and passed him, and they went down the stairs. She heard her door close, looked round, and he was following them.

Marie could have been the best player in the world – or the worst. Charlotte didn't know, for she heard nothing, but she clapped when the others did, and it was like being in a dream, suspended from all reality, sitting there pretending to listen, and Jared only a few feet away. When Marie's little recital was over Charlotte stood up and walked quietly away, melting into the shadows, unnoticed by anyone. She needed desperately to be alone, to have time to think. Was this just another episode in the difficult series of days through which she was living? But how – why – could a man be so deliberately cruel as to pretend an emotion he didn't feel? She had seen his face, seen the pain in his eyes as he told her certain words that implied— Charlotte paused. She was well into the shadows now, well away from the villa, and surrounded by trees and shrubs. And no one to see. What had his words implied? That he loved her. And because of them she had foolishly opened her mouth and admitted – she put her hand to her face in utter, overwhelming dismay. 'Oh no,' she whispered. 'Oh no—'

'Why did you run away?'

She whirled round at the sound of his voice. Outlined in the very faint lights that showed from the villa, Jared stood there watching her. There was nowhere to run, because she didn't know the grounds and could see nothing save a distant glow from the house.

'I want to think,' she whispered.

He walked towards her, and she remained where she was, despite her instinct to flee. 'Charlotte,' he began, 'I want to talk.'

'No. There's – there's nothing to say—'

'There is. There's a lot – a great deal,' and he put his hand out to touch her face, and said in a tone of wonder: 'Why are there tears on your cheeks?'

'I don't – there's n-nothing to talk about,' she stammered.

'Yes, there is. Beginning with why I ran away from you two years ago.'

With a wordless cry of pain she turned from him, unable to bear any more, uncaring that the darkness was complete and all-enveloping, only knowing that she could not hear any more of those words. And he caught her, and held her, and turned her round to face him.

'Please,' he said. 'Please let me tell you.'

She was helpless in his grip. His strength was great; although his grasp was a gentle one, she knew he would not release her.

'You're hurting me,' she whispered.

'No, I'm not, I'm being very careful not to. I've hurt you enough – I won't do so any more – ever.'

'Oh, please – Jared, it doesn't matter – I don't – you

mustn't—' she didn't know what she was saying, but she didn't want to *hear* anything.

'It does matter – and I must, Charlotte. I love you – can you hear that? I *love* you.'

'Oh no!' She began to laugh helplessly, tears streaming down her face as the tension finally broke.

Then he kissed her. He kissed her so effectively that the laughter was stilled, and became a murmur of protest, which died away almost immediately, and then he didn't need to hold her any more, because Charlotte reached up to put her arms round his neck as his own arms enfolded her tightly and held her as if he would never let her free.

Two black silhouettes merging into one, and the only witness, a wide-awake owl perched in a tree beside them who suddenly flew away with an ear-piercing shriek, and the shadows moved, and Jared whispered in Charlotte's ear: 'Don't run away.'

'I couldn't if I tried,' she whispered back. 'You're holding me too tightly.'

'Good. Then you've got to listen to me.'

'I suppose so.' But she wanted to – now.

'I met you in Paris two long years ago – and I've thought of you ever since – oh, I know you won't believe me, but my dear one, it is quite true. I was a wanderer then, a nomad, restless and unsettled, and searching for something – or someone, I knew not what. Then I saw you standing there all alone, a lost little girl, and I knew I'd found what I'd been looking for.' He moved his hand to caress the back of her neck, and it was just right. 'Listen to me well. I said a little girl – and that is what you were, and still are in many ways. Charlotte, I'm thirty-five – I'm fourteen years older than you.' He paused, as if he had just said something so terrible that she would have to respond to it. She did.

'Is that all?' she said.

'All?' he groaned. 'No, it's not, but it's enough. Then – I was not prepared to be enmeshed by any woman. I was free, my own man. I'm a very reluctant vineyard owner, as you may have noticed. My plan was to wait until Marie was old enough to take over and leave her to it. Was – until a week or so ago.' He stopped again and buried his face in her neck. 'Oh, God, what's the matter with me? The words aren't coming out right at all.'

'Yes, they are. I'm listening,' she responded simply.

'No one will ever know my thoughts when I came out of the stable and saw you standing there – I didn't know what I felt myself – only that I was shaken beyond all understanding. And I hit out, because my own reaction frightened me. Everything was all tidied up in my mind. You'd been put to the back of it – although you were always there, because I couldn't help it – and I wanted you to go away.'

'I know that. Oh yes, I know that,' she whispered, and began to shake.

He held her closely. 'Do I frighten you, Charlotte?'

'Not – not any more. Don't let me go.'

'No, I won't. Oh, love, my love, I ache all over for you. Life has been hell for me – but it's no use fighting you any more. When I played that tune, I knew—' He kissed her, then his face was wet with her tears, and in a husky voice he said: 'Tell me something. Does Aunt Marie know? Have you told her anything?'

'Everything,' she answered.

'Ah!' he gave a deep sigh, then began, most surprisingly, to laugh. 'Ah yes, *now* I see.'

'I don't understand.' She was puzzled, but not too much so, because there was that comfortable feeling that everything was going to be all right, and it was the most wonderful sensation in the world.

'Sorry, my love. I'll tell you. Two years ago – after that meeting – I came down here because I needed someone to talk to. Only I found I couldn't tell her anything, but that tune – *our* tune – was stuck in my head, and I found myself playing it on that same guitar constantly until it even drove Aunt Marie mad. So now we both know why she asked me to play tonight, don't we?'

'You mean – you think she *knows*?'

'I think she's known all along. She must be far cleverer than I am.'

'Haven't you forgotten something?' The image of Margot's face was disturbingly before Charlotte all of a sudden. 'You already have someone.'

'Margot?' Even in the darkness she sensed his smile. 'That has been fading fast for a while. We both knew it—'

'Then why do you and Paul dislike one another so, if you're not jealous?'

'Paul hates *me* – I was indifferent to *him* until I saw you in his arms. Then I was jealous, but it was not because of Margot, it was because of *you*, in the same way that I saw red when Yves kissed you outside the stables. I wanted to kill him there and then – and I'm not a jealous person as a rule. That was when I suspected I was fighting a losing battle – against you, my love.'

He gave a deep sigh. 'Oh, God, it's good to get it all out in the open at last. Do you know something? I bought you a little present yesterday. You remember the ring you tried on?'

'You didn't – you bought it?'

He laughed. 'Don't sound so surprised. You're going to be showered with them from now on. That's just a start—'

'Oh yes. My present for Aunt Marie, the pendant. You came to an arrangement with James about that, didn't you?'

He gave a gasp of mock dismay. 'You're too shrewd for me. What am I going to do with you? There's only one solution that I can see. And can you guess what that is?'

She could, but she wanted to hear it. 'No,' she answered.

'Come into the light. I want to see your face when I ask you.'

'No. I like it here,' and she smiled up at him.

'I can see enough,' he said softly. 'Will you marry me, and live at the château?'

'Yes. The first time I went into that room, it was as if I was going home – it was the oddest feeling, Jared.'

'But a true one. It will be your home for as long as you want it to be, my dearest Charlotte. You know, I had planned it that when Marie was old enough I would leave, and go round the world – but somehow the idea no longer appeals – I wonder why?'

'I don't know.' She reached up to stroke his face. 'What about Madame Grenier? I don't think she'll be very pleased with this.'

'She'll learn to live with it. We get along well enough – we respect one another, but there's not much affection between us. The main thing binding us together is Marie – we both love her. And you do too, don't you?'

'Yes.'

'It will be all right, you'll see. Aunt Heloise has a high regard for you. I know that already. And as for Aunt Marie—' he paused, and began to laugh softly. 'Oh, I can't wait to see her face. What a birthday present we have for her, eh, Charlotte? Come now, we'll go and tell her – though I suspect she might well know already.'

The guests had departed, Marie had gone to bed. Aunt Marie waited on the terrace for them, and as they walked slowly towards her, hand in hand, she lifted her arms.

'Oh, my dears,' she said. 'My dear children. Come into the light, I want to see your faces.'

They stood before her, and she indicated a bottle of champagne by her side.

'Tell me,' she said, her voice softened, 'have we a reason for opening this now?'

'Oh yes, my dear cunning aunt, we have, thanks to you, and a certain tune,' and Jared bent to kiss her. 'Will you be well enough to go to a wedding in a few weeks' time?'

'Will I?' Her laughter echoed around the pool, a joyous sound. 'Let them try to stop me!' A startled dragonfly skimmed the surface of the water and vanished into the night as the champagne cork popped and the three of them drank their toast. Over the glasses, Charlotte and Jared looked at one another, and he raised his and said softly:

'Dreams never grow old – and we have many more years of dreaming ahead of us.' She didn't need to answer. The love shone in her eyes, and was matched by that in his own.

OMNIBUS — The 3 in 1 HARLEQUIN
only $1.75 per volume

Here is a great new exciting idea from Harlequin. THREE GREAT ·ROMANCES — complete and unabridged — BY THE SAME AUTHOR — in one deluxe paperback volume — for the unbelievably low price of only $1.75 per volume.

We have chosen some of the finest works of four world-famous authors . . .

CATHERINE AIRLIE

VIOLET WINSPEAR ②

KATHRYN BLAIR

ROSALIND BRETT

. . . and reprinted them in the 3 in 1 Omnibus. Almost 600 pages of pure entertainment for just $1.75 each. A TRULY "JUMBO" READ!

These four Harlequin Omnibus volumes are now available. The following pages list the exciting novels by each author.

Climb aboard the Harlequin Omnibus now! The coupon below is provided for your convenience in ordering.

Catherine Airlie

Omnibus

An author whose very fine work has become famous throughout North America, and greatly anticipated by readers of romance all over the world. The three stories chosen for this volume highlight her unusual talent of combining the elements of compassion and suspense in one exceptional novel.

. . . . CONTAINING:

DOCTOR OVERBOARD . . . on board a luxury liner, cruising between the Canary Islands, Trinidad and Barbados, a young Scot, Mairi Finlay, is facing a traumatic experience, torn between her growing affection for the young ship's surgeon, and her duty to her employer who has set her an impossible task . . . (#979).

NOBODY'S CHILD . . . from London England, we are taken to a mediaeval castle, the Schloss Lamberg, situated on the outskirts of the City of Vienna, to brush shoulders with the aristocracy of the music world. Amidst all of this beauty, a young girl, Christine Dainton, is submerged in the romance of a lifetime with one of the most admired men in the world . . . (#1258).

A WIND SIGHING . . . Jean Lorimer's life has always been happy here, on the small Hebridean Island of Kinnail, owned by the Lorimer family for centuries. Now, Jean and her mother are grief stricken on the death of her father. They will surely lose their home too, for Kinnail was always inherited by the eldest male in the family, whose arrival they expect any day now (#1328).

$1.75 per volume

Kathryn Blair

Omnibus

Kathryn Blair's outstanding work has become famous and most appreciated by those who seek real-life characters against backgrounds which create and hold the interest throughout the entire story, thus producing the most captivating and memorable romantic novels available today.

. . . . CONTAINING:

DOCTOR WESTLAND . . . Tess Carlen is invited to recuperate in Tangier after suffering almost fatal injuries in an accident. On the voyage, Tess agrees to look after a small boy, and to deliver him to his father on arrival. By doing so, Tess becomes deeply embroiled in the mystery of Tangier which cloaks Dr. Philip Westland and his young son . . . (#954).

BATTLE OF LOVE . . . on the death of her husband, Catherine and her small son are offered a home by her father-in-law, Leon Verender, co-guardian of the boy. Chaos develops rapidly between them, caused by conflicting ideas on how to raise a child. Leon's scheming fiancée then delivers an ultimatum to Catherine—making life for her and her son impossible . . . (#1038).

FLOWERING WILDERNESS . . . a rubber plantation in Africa was no place for a woman as far as David Raynor was concerned. Nicky Graham had a great deal of courage, and she was determined to stay. Alas, before long, Nicky was forced to leave, but now, she was very much in love with the same David Raynor . . . (#1148).

$1.75 per volume

Rosalind Brett

Omnibus

A writer with an excitingly different appeal which transports the reader on a journey of enchantment to far off places where warm, human people live in true to life circumstances. Miss Brett's refreshing touch to the age-old story of love, continues to fascinate her ever-increasing number of faithful readers.

. . . . CONTAINING:

THE GIRL AT WHITE DRIFT . . . Jerry Lake had travelled from England to Canada to live with her unknown guardian, Dave Farren. On arrival, Mr. Farren drove Jerry to his home, White Drift Farm, explaining that a few months' farm life would strengthen and build a fine body. To her utter horror, Jerry realized that this man thought she was a boy! . . . (#1101).

WINDS OF ENCHANTMENT . . . in Kanos, Africa, in surroundings of intense heat, green thick jungle, insects and fever, Pat Brading faces the heartbreak of losing her father. The acute depression and shock which she suffers in the following months, gradually subsides, and slowly she becomes aware that she is now married to a man who revolts her, and whom she must, somehow, escape . . . (#1176).

BRITTLE BONDAGE . . . when Venetia wrote the letter which had brought Blake Garrard immediately to her side in a time of need, she had felt great sorrow and bewilderment. Now, some time and a great deal of pain later, it was the contents of another letter which must drive her away from him. Only now, Blake was her husband . . . (#1319).

$1.75 per volume